Mercy of Hell Hollow

By Marnie Reynolds-Bourque

Dedicated to Mercy, my late great, great, grandmother.

It is my hope this book humanizes your daughter and

deflates the legend so she can rest in peace.

And to my husband for his endless support.

Marnie Reynolds-Bourque

To request permissions, please contact the author at artistmarnie@yahoo.com

Paperback ISBN: 978-1-7344145-7-8

Ebook ISBN: 978-1-7344145-9-2

First paperback edition

Edited by: Perry Iles

Cover art by Marnie Reynolds-Bourque

Lucky 7 Publishing, Sterling, Ct

Artistmarnie.com

Please note this is my interpretation of events that took place well over 100 years ago, and I have taken liberties with this book. The Grange, Pachaug Forest, and Ellis Island all came about a few years later than when mentioned in this book. To further my story, I used artistic license and earlier dates.

Prologue

March 1983, Pachaug Forest

The music blared from the boombox, shattering the peace of the forest. A substantial fire crackled and sparked, its bright yellow and orange fingers reaching into the night sky. The campfire illuminated the teenagers gathered around it, warming them in the process.

A few teenagers took long pulls of beer from the bottles in their hands. Couples huddled together, kissing. Others stood and talked. They were all bonded together, their camaraderie bolstered by alcohol and the prospect of tempting a witch.

One lanky boy stood and walked to the blazing fire. He looked like he was simply staring into it, but then a stream of urine glittered in the light of the flames. He relieved himself quickly and on the edge of the fire as to not disturb the strength of the flames.

"Now you're really pushing it, Joe," Heather chortled. The others laughed too, or yelled encouragement.

"I want to see if the legend is true. If she really is a witch, that should really piss her off," Joe said. He finished, zipped his pants and stepped away from the fire to return to where he had been sitting.

"What legend?" A girl sitting around the fire asked.

"You're kidding, right?" Joe asked her. "That circle of stones in front of you is a grave marker for a witch. There are different stories. Some say she was murdered and haunts the woods, and some say she is just a witch. I just know that if you mess with her grave something bad will happen to you. I know a few kids that had car accidents after messing with it. Or their house burned down."

"I had no idea! Aren't you afraid?" The girl asked Joe, her eyes wide, pulling her coat around her as if against a sudden chill.

"Nope. I don't believe in witches, but I do like taking chances," he said with a laugh, as he returned to his spot around the fire.

The teenagers resumed their conversations. Laughter bubbled as they drank more, and they spent a few more hours around the bonfire. It grew late, and they tipped their heads back, drinking the last of their alcohol before throwing the empty bottles and cans on the ground or into the fire. They walked to their cars, yelling farewells to each other. Car doors slammed, adding more noise, then there was the crunch of tires digging into the gravel road. The noise of the engines echoed through the woods, seeming to rupture the night. Taillights eventually disappeared, leaving long, fresh scars in the dirt and new ruts in the gravel road. The kids left without a care, the fire still glowing, litter and beer bottles scattered across the clearing.

The flames eventually petered out and the forest slowly returned to the habitual quiet it had been enjoying before it was so rudely disrupted.

One hundred years earlier…

Saturday, March 14th, 1883

I shiver within my coat as the wind tries to blow straight through me. The grass sparkles with frost as I stand alongside the other mourners at the small grave. The sky overhead is a dismal gray, and it looks like it'll snow soon. The only sounds that break the stark silence are the cawing of the crows in the trees and the heartbreaking sobs of a mother, distraught, being held up by her husband while she grieves for her young son.

It's painful to witness, and I look down at the little hands within mine and the two small figures on each side of me, and then over at my little daughter being held in my husband's arms, to reassure myself my brood is intact and well.

I look up and see my husband doing the same review of our children, and our eyes meet. No word passes between us to break the quiet, but it doesn't take words to make me realize that we're both feeling grateful it's not us up there, standing in front of the grave.

Diphtheria made its rounds in our town again during this long winter, and collected many souls. It's a terrible illness, and children catch it easily. Their sore, swollen throats make it hard for them to breathe, and the victim often chokes to death. Or they perish when they can no longer take a breath. It is a torturous, slow illness and I am grateful that my children have been spared. I hope they always will be.

I turn my gaze back to the scene in front of me and look up to the gray sky, devoid of any sunlight. I've always thought it should be a dismal, rainy day when you are saying goodbye to a loved one. It's appropriate, somehow. My husband never agrees with me. He says if it were true it would always be raining. I see what he means, but I'm still grateful for overcast funerals. The dreariness brings me comfort.

Little Robert was just five years old; his parents' only child. Although the loss of any child is horrific, it must be worse when it's your only child. When that lone child departs, he takes so much from your life with him. Now there's only silence, and the absence of any possibility of grandchildren.

My heart breaks for poor Louise.

We stand to one side of this melancholy little group, surrounding the gaping hole in the earth and the little coffin that is set beside it. Louise and her husband are of course somberly dressed, as are the rest of us. She is a lovely, kind woman who doesn't deserve this. But then who does?

The pastor is delivering words that are meant to comfort us all, but it is hard to hear over Louise's weeping. The Pastor, a kindly man, finishes his reading, closes his bible and holds it close to his chest, taking comfort from it himself. It cannot be an easy task, officiating at a young child's interment. And he's had to do it so often.

The crowd at the cemetery is large enough, which is nice in terms of support for the bereaved, but honestly, I wonder if Louise and her husband will even remember who attended and who didn't. Grief will turn this awful occasion into little more than a blur. Is that a good thing? Do you want to remember every second of something like this?

I would think not.

I look again at the tops of my little boys' heads, hidden under thick woven caps, and I grip their hands more firmly. I must keep them close to protect them from this fearful sight.

Oh, the questions we will have after this, I think to myself. We believe in the almighty, but why must he take the children? The Pastor would no doubt say he has a reason, but I can't see one, not while I'm looking at Louise sobbing in her husband's arms.

Clearing his throat, the Pastor finishes the formal part of the service and says a few words about little Robert, who was of course a lovely little boy. He never had the chance to become anything else. The pastor tells us Robert is now with the Lord, and says a few more platitudes that are meant to comfort us, but I am having a hard time finding solace in anything he says. The dismal little ceremony is mercifully brief, and as the coffin is lowered into the ground the sobbing intensifies and my heart feels heavier than ever. My boys look at me, and I release one hand to place my finger to my lips, in a silent motion. I will speak with them later, and I don't want their high little voices breaking the quiet. There is the thud of dirt hitting wood, and this continues for a while, a background cadence like the slow footsteps of some greater being as we silently walk from the gravesite and head to our wagons. Most of us will now go to the nearby church for refreshments after this ghastly ceremony.

As we leave the cemetery with the others, I look back to watch the men continuing to fill the grave, while Louise and her husband stare at the place where their child will now remain forever.

Who created these terrible illnesses that take such little souls? The same good Lord who must now give Louise and her husband comfort, because I'm sure none of us can.

Friday, May 4th, 1883

The delicate scent of lilacs carries into my bedroom through the slightly open window. I take a deep breath, inhaling the lovely smell with my eyes still closed. I open them eventually and roll over to sit on the edge of the bed. The other side is empty. Gibby must be already up, probably stoking the fire for my little cook stove to make breakfast.

I rise from my warm bed, my swollen belly making me ungainly and unsteady on my feet. I make my bed and fold the Afghan my grandmother Antonia made for me. She always told me that having a heavy blanket is like having ten ordinary blankets because of its weight, and she's right as usual. The blanket's weight on me is like a hug from Grandma Antonia herself, and it makes me think of her with gratitude when the blanket keeps Gibby and me warm during the cold, dark winter nights.

The curtains flutter at my window as I walk to my wardrobe to find a dress to wear for the day. Shivering a bit from the morning chill, I remove my nightgown as quickly as possible and place it inside our tall wardrobe. I take out a chemise and a cornflower blue dress, which is a little higher in the front because of my condition, as I have let out many of the seams to make room for my ever-expanding belly. My mother taught me to sew, and this hard-learned skill is beneficial because we don't have many places to purchase finished clothing out here.

I finish dressing for the day, and glimpse at myself in my small mirror. The face gazing back at me has green eyes and even teeth set in a small smile. My light brown hair is in disarray from sleeping, so I gather it back into a bun, and then go through to the kitchen, where as I suspected, Gibby is in front of the cookstove stoking it.

"Morning," he greets me.

"And a good morning to you," I reply, enjoying the warmth of the fire as I make for the cupboard. I smile at my husband as I gather the things I need to make breakfast.

Gibby is a stocky man with a long beard that keeps his face warm during the winter months. Lately he has started wearing it during the warmer months as well, much to my chagrin. He smiles back at me, making the mustache above his lip jiggle as it always does when his lips turn up. He is wearing black trousers and a linen shirt I sewed for him.

He watches me as I pull out my ruffled apron, place the hoop over my head, and try to reach behind me to tie the loose ends. This belly of mine protrudes and gets in the way of everything, so an apron is indispensable. I feel him at my back as he takes the ends from me and ties the apron securely.

"Thank you, Gibby. What are your plans for today?" I ask him, continuing to prepare our breakfast.

Gibby turns from me and walks to his chair, where he sits. I know from the silence that he is preparing his pipe. I turn to see his cheeks puff a few times, then smoke floats upwards from it, forming a cloud near his head. The smoke and fragrance remind me of my Papa, who also enjoys a good smoke.

"I'll take care of the livestock, then I'll finishing cutting our firewood," he answers, as I continue on, now cracking a couple of eggs and adding them to the cast iron skillet on my little stove.

Stacking and cutting firewood is a never-ending chore. There is just never enough wood. Wood is our main source of heat, and during the winter it is sorely needed so we can all survive. We are blessed to have quite a bit of land from which to harvest wood, and often Gibby will sell some of it to those who aren't as fortunate as ourselves.

As the eggs cook in the pan, I cut some bread into slices, butter them, and place them on plates to go with the eggs. There is something wonderful about providing a meal for your family, and it fills me with joy to do so. As I wipe my hands on my apron I look up to see my twin boys come galloping into our kitchen.

Bert is the older twin, and he's always the leader in their escapades. Earl is the worrier, the follower. They are as different in temperament as they are similar in looks, and they're quite boisterous, in the way of all boys everywhere. Their heads are covered with thick chestnut hair, and they peer at me with bright hazel eyes, which seem to be a Reynolds trait. They've just rolled out of bed, and their matching cowlicks stand straight up, creating a humorous sight this morning and making me smile. Born in the winter of 1879, they are now just a little over four years old.

"Whoa," Gibby says as they fly by him. "How about you take a seat at the table and wait for your breakfast?" Freshly awakened and rejuvenated from their rest, they smile at me as they do as he says.

"Yes, sir," the twins' little voices answer in unison. I notice that they are still in their nightshirts, with socks on their little feet. Cool mornings mean chilly floors, and the cold floor has taught them to keep their socks on after they get up.

"Is Mary Alice awake too?" I ask them, knowing that the loud antics of the twins can awaken the dead from their slumber, never mind a very active three-year-old who is always ready to go.

"She is still sleeping, Mama," Bert replies. At his response, Gibby stands to go and get her so we can break our fast together.

After breakfast, Gibby heads out to our barn to get our horse and wagon ready. While he does this, the boys bring our plates to me and we wash up together, then I help all the children get dressed for the day.

Once dressed in our clothes and coats, we walk outside into the bright yard to wait for our wagon ride to begin. Some of us wait patiently. The boys are off exploring everything around them, but Mary Alice remains standing close to my skirts as she is still learning to walk, never mind run with these hooligans.

I pick Mary Alice up, enjoying the closeness of holding my daughter. I know these moments of clinging to my skirts will be short-lived, as I watch my two eldest children run circles around me with no desire whatsoever to be picked up. Soon enough Mary Alice will join them, and I will have three little ruffians to oversee. But until then, I enjoy her being dependent upon my security.

Gibby soon pulls up alongside us, and the horse tosses his head about, his thick mane rippling along his strong neck, anxious to get going, a sentiment shared by the twins. Smokey is large and black, with three stockinged feet and a calm temperament. He has a large stall in our barn, along with a cow named Bessie and some chickens that roam the barnyard too.

Gibby appears at my side and helps us into the wagon. The twins go in the back, and Mary Alice stays in my arms as she is a bit young to be let loose in the wagon all by herself. The twins are more than enough to keep an eye on as they reach for some low-hanging branch or something else that catches their curiosity.

We start on the hill that goes up from our property, passing a row of tall trees. Our town and the surrounding towns don't have much wooded areas as the wood is needed for heat or to build homes and furniture. So to have tall trees on one's property is a blessing indeed. It's like having money in the bank.

As we travel, I start to think about the origin of the name Hell Hollow. Who ever thought to give a road a curse-word? Or that I could ever live on such a road? Gibby and I are not sure of the origin of the name, but his suspicions are that it reflected the frustration of an earlier farmer who went through hell trying to make a farm here. The soil is terrible, and there's far too many rocks. It would be hell for a farmer. Its cuss-word name and rocky land were probably the main reasons why we were able to purchase it so advantageously

We travel up the road in shade of the tall trees that tower over us. At the top, Gibby turns Smokey to the left onto another smaller road not much traveled, and parks the wagon.

Wood cutting is a painstaking task. Chopping the tree, cutting the wood into lengths, sharpening the ax as needed, then stacking the wood into his wagon and restacking it at our house. Sometimes when Gibby sells the wood he has to stack it all over again at the customer's home. Not everyone is fit to stack the wood on their homesteads. Some are elderly and can't do much, and some are wealthy and don't want the bother.

Gibby has a lot of patience and endurance with the task at hand. Sometimes I wonder how he does not go mad with the monotony of it all. But he is a strong, solid man who never gives up providing for his family. A benefit besides the coin we receive is that the firewood cutting task keeps him in prime condition, which is a good thing when you have a farm and a family to raise.

The children and I leave Gibby to his task and walk slowly through the forest. Wherever we look, the branches are tipped with pink, ready to burst into leaf. Soon the woods will be alive with color, shade, and life. After a short walk, I call out to the twins that it's time to return home.

We say our temporary goodbyes to Gibby, but our parting is interrupted by the sound of hooves approaching, breaking the quiet of the woods. The hoof beats come closer until a white horse gallops into view, and we know by the horse that it's Jasper O'Dowd, our neighbor to the west. Jasper halts in front of us and tips his cap in welcome. An immigrant from Ireland, he and his wife are good friends of ours.

"Top of the morning to you," he greets us as his horse trots in place for a few seconds. It rolls its eyes, anxious to be home. Jasper still has an Irish way about him, something some of the other town residents don't care much care for, but Gibby and I pay no mind to. I'm always puzzled at the way some people have no tolerance for people who are a bit different from themselves.

"Good morning Jasper! And how are you this fine spring day?" Gibby asks.

"On my way home from picking up some seeds from the post office. Lookin' to grow a new variety of corn as well as the usual pumpkins."

Gibby and I know that Jasper's land is hell to farm, like ours. Both men do the best with what they have.

Jasper and his wife Cora have two boys themselves: Frederick who is five, and Samuel a year younger, both of them close in age to our twins.

"Shall I drop the seeds off at home and then come back and give you a hand? You know what they say – many hands make lighter work," Jasper smiles at Gibby.

"I'm obliged to you, Jasper, but I don't have much left to do apart from loading the wagon and stacking the wood back at home. Keep the favor for when I truly need it." Gibby replies.

"Well, I'll be on my way then. Let's get the families together soon," Jasper says, smiling his bright smile.

"That sounds wonderful," I reply. "Say hello to Cora for me, and be sure and tell her I'd love to see her soon."

"I surely will," Jasper says. He tips his hat again and spurs his anxious mount into motion.

Gibby returns to loading the wagon, and I call the twins to start our walk home. We walk leisurely, alternating with carrying Mary Alice on my hip – at least what I have of a hip these days –and letting her walk beside me.

We turn a corner, and our home comes into view. It is a typical period style building, rectangular with four windows along the front and door in the middle. Stone stairs divide the stone wall that runs along the front into equal lengths, leading up to our front door. Some of the larger stones for the steps and the walkway came from our friends the Culvers who have a quarry up on Pine Hill. Buying our stone is how we first met, and we soon became fast friends.

The smell of lilacs soon surrounds us, putting a smile on my face as it always does. When we first moved into Hell Hollow, our neighbor further down the road, Mrs. Gordon, offered us lots of shrubs. She had an abundance of them, and she was right generous.

When we get to the yard, the twins take off like a shot to the barn to check on the cow and chickens. The boys reach the chicken shed first, and each grabs his own basket from hooks set at their height to gather eggs.

As the chickens squawk and flap about, Mary Alice clings to me. The chickens scare her with the racket they're making. Adding to the chickens' agitation, the boys whoop in excitement whenever they find an egg. The twins set their eggs in their baskets with surprising delicacy and count them.

"I have four!" says Earl.

Not to be outdone, Bert counts his own eggs. "So do I!" He shouts. I sigh with relief. At least I won't have to listen to them bicker about who has the most eggs. Praise be for small mercies!

"Great job counting, boys!" I tell them with a smile.

Earl closes the door carefully as we back out of the pen and return to the house with our bounty. We pass a large lilac bush hiding a good sized privy, with a wisteria vine climbing the side. The wisteria will take over masking the ungodly smells when the lilac blooms fade. Thankfully, today there is only the lovely scent of lilacs.

"Boys, do you need to use the privy?" I ask the twins, as they walk right on past the small building.

"No Mama," Bert answers, with a mischievous smile, and runs off. I sigh as I know he has relieved himself somewhere out in the woods. Although they are right equipped to go anywhere they please, I like to try to instill some decency in them.

Earl, the easier-going twin, sets his basket down and disappears inside, and the door slams behind him. I holler to Bert to wait one minute for his brother, and he tears back to my side till his cohort returns. Bert rarely uses the privy, as any old tree or shrub will do just as nicely, to my distress. A loud bang interrupts my thoughts as Earl comes out and gathers his basket, and the four of us carry on to the rear of our house.

The twins place their baskets down on the kitchen table and I tell them to get their slates and practice their letters. They take Mary Alice to the parlor, where they will do as I asked while she plays with her blocks.

After placing the latest batch of eggs in my ice box, I glance around the kitchen to see what else needs to be taken care of. The sound of hooves breaks the silence, and I look out to see Gibby out by the barn, next to the area where he will stack his wood. Knowing it will take him a little while to accomplish his task, I head into the parlor where I see the boys sitting nicely on the floor, their little heads bowed over their slates as they work, while Mary Alice stacks her little blocks. I walk to my chair, place my feet upon my footstool and enjoy the calm.

Saturday, May 5th, 1883

"Can we have our midday meal then leave for town?" Gibby calls out to me.

"Sure." I nod my head in agreement, anxious not to say too much that will get the children too excited about our trip into town. I am enjoying my few minutes of peace, sitting in my chair in our little parlor this morning, with the children practicing their letters again. I don't have much energy these last few days, and experience tells me I'm nearing my time to deliver.

But the twins' heads have popped up at the word "town" and I can see their hazel eyes widen with excitement. Broad smiles appear, showing their happiness at our impending trip.

The boys jump to their feet, delighted to be going on an adventure, and my quiet moment vanishes like a wisp of smoke disappearing into the air. A trip into town is a big event, as the children usually get some penny candy, and Gibby and I will catch up on the latest news and events.

Seeing the children's faces light up in anticipation, I rise to my feet and go to the kitchen to take leftover chicken and potato salad out of the ice box

Working quickly I set the table, filling glasses of milk for the children and glasses of water for Gibby and me before calling everyone through to the kitchen to eat. No sooner do the words escape my mouth than the boys run in, with Mary Alice toddling behind. Gibby follows with a smile on his face, no doubt hungry from his morning's chores. He and I sit in our chairs, while the children sit together on a bench that runs along the side of the table.

Soon the only sounds are of people eating and the tinkling of forks scraping plates, which is a lovely sound to my ears. Many families go without in our town, as times are tough, and I am always pleased that Gibby and I can provide well for our growing family.

With everyone anxious to go to town, the cold chicken disappears quickly. While the boys and I tidy up from lunch, Gibby heads to the parlor, where he will most likely take a quick nap as he usually does. I swear that man could fall asleep on a picket fence, and it's an ability that makes me feel envious. Even a short nap will leave him refreshed, and knowing this I slow a bit with my chores to give him a few extra moments of rest.

Once we finish cleaning up, the boys take off to the parlor while I take down my dog eared copy of *Aunt Babette's Cookbook* from a shelf. It's my only cookbook, and it's getting worn out. The edges are torn, there are handwritten notes in the margins, and it's bulging with additional recipes added inside under relevant sections. The book is well-used and well-loved, stained with occasional kitchen spillages. I got it from my mother, and it has taught me much in a short time about preparing food for my husband and family. It looks like what it is, a vital kitchen accessory.

I peruse a few recipes, and once I've chosen a favorite I write down the ingredients I will need for the Culvers' visit as well as meals for our family over the coming week. When I'm finished, I close the book, place it back in its spot on the shelf and glance around my kitchen, to confirm everything is in its place. Satisfied everything is in order, I join the rest of my family in the parlor.

As I expected, Gibby is in his chair, his mouth open, snoring softly. Walking past him to my own chair, I sit down, as he has only been asleep a short time and I feel bad waking him so soon. The children are absorbed with their letters, practicing on their slates, so I help them for a bit, to let their father get his rest.

After a short time I ask Mary Alice to wake her Papa. She walks over to him and climbs very gently into his lap. I have learned to ask her to wake him when needed, because I know the twins will give him a fright, which will irritate him. Mary Alice is the better choice. I wouldn't want to be woken from a restful slumber by someone jumping and yelling at me, and I believe Gibby is very grateful for my choice, as he awakens with a smile rather than a horrified look.

Gibby continues to smile at Mary Alice as he gently places her on the floor, then stands. He stretches his hands high above his head, lengthening his torso in a satisfying stretch. I watch as his suspenders do their job of keeping his pants in place at his waist rather than piled around his ankles, which would not be a good thing at all, and smile at him. He finishes his stretch and winks at me.

"Are you boys ready to head to town?" He asks the twins. "Or would you rather stack some wood?"

The twins look at him, then me, unsure of what to answer, as they were told we were going into town instead of doing chores.

Gibby sees their worried expressions. "Don't worry, boys, we are heading into town," he says, at which the twins jump up, happy that there are no chores for them.

Smiling, we walk to the rear of the house to where our jackets hang. Even though it is warming up, it can get cool on the long and exposed ride to town. Once the children are bundled up, I grab a blanket from the parlor that the children can use in the wagon if they get chilly. Gibby joins us after retrieving his money pouch and we head out the back door to Smokey and our waiting wagon.

We leave Hell Hollow Road and turn onto the main road called Ekonk Hill. Ekonk is the English version of the Native American name "Egunk", which means "long hill" in the local dialect. And Ekonk Hill is certainly a long hill. Before we had children, Gibby and I used to ride up there at sunset and watch for shooting stars from the ridge. Plenty of wagons and carriages would be up there on starry moonlit nights, keeping a respectful distance from each other – no doubt because not all of the parked carriages contained married couples.

Most of the land around town has been cleared for homes and firewood, and you can see for miles from the top of the long hillside, making it a very scenic vista. There are a few lucky homesteads along this ridge, well-placed to enjoy the beautiful sunsets the hill provides.

Rolling along, we wave to people out in their yards and soon reach the intersection that will take us to the little town of Oneco. Gibby guides Smokey onto the wide road that runs east to Rhode Island or west into the towns of Moosup and Plainfield, and farther on the state Capitol, Hartford, a place I have never been to, as I tend to stick to visiting Rhode Island.

Oneco consists of the general store, Whitford's, the Flying Owl Tavern and a few smaller taverns, and the Oneco Mill. The Oneco Mill employs most of the people in the town, along with the Sterling Finishing Mill, located a short distance away in Sterling. There are more mills in the neighboring town of Moosup, and they employ French Canadian immigrants as well as local folk.

Smokey keeps up a steady pace, and the wagon wheels turn smoothly along the well-worn road. The day is warm for spring, and as we travel, Smokey's hooves kick up dust from the dry road surface and we see the grass starting to turn a deeper green.

Whitford's is a large general store, and its white-painted walls make it stand out as a landmark in the town, an institution of sorts. It's a meeting place, a post office, and a great source of provisions. Mr. Whitford sells pretty much anything a family needs on a day-to-day basis, as well as other items that might be a bit harder to find.

Gibby pulls Smokey over onto the side of the road, jumps from the wagon and gathers the horse's reins to secure them to the hitching post.

Once I am safely on the ground, Mary Alice toddles over to me. I grab her hand and we walk as a family toward the staircase leading up and into the store. Climbing the stairs is no easy feat in my condition, and when I reach the top I have to take a minute to catch my breath, so I stand and read the large board that hangs beside the front doors, covered with local announcements. The board is full of different-sized papers that overlap each other, bearing handwritten advertisements from townsfolk selling items, townsfolk looking for work or just general announcements.

A notice advertising dinner and dancing at the new Grange catches my eye, and I take note of the June date. The baby should be here by then, and it will be a nice time to see our neighbors and introduce the new addition to the family.

A loud crash interrupts my thoughts, and I move as quickly as my condition allows into the store to see what trouble my boys have gotten into this time. Thankfully all they've done is knock over a small display of canned beans. I feel very lucky indeed, as last time they broke a jar of pickles, and we had to buy them. I start to bend over to straighten the display when I feel Gibby's hand upon my back.

"Thank you", I say smiling at him, as he starts to fix the display.

"Come over here, boys. I reckon you've done enough damage to Mr. Whitford's store already," I admonish the twins. The boys come to my side and bend to help their father straighten the cans. Once they are back in place, we walk toward the candy area, twins in tow with their heads bowed in shame.

"Sorry about my boys, Mr. Whitford," I say as I reach the candy counter, with Mr. Whitford behind it. "And how are you this fine morning?"

Mr. Whitford is a tall, thin man with a large mustache and wire-rimmed spectacles over kind, twinkling eyes. He is wearing an apron as most shopkeepers do, to keep his clothes clean and to let anyone entering the store know who's in charge here.

"I'm doing well, Mrs. Reynolds, thank you kindly. I see you have brought me lots of company today, and I hope my candy selection will be to their liking," he responds with a smile.

The candy section of Whitford's glows like a rainbow on a cloudy day as the sun illuminates it through the tall windows. Mr. Whitford knows what he is doing by placing the candy directly in the spotlight. The glass containers hold lots of brightly wrapped and loose candy, as well as chocolate candy – which he'll have to move into the shade if the sun gets much hotter. It is a sparkling and colorful palette of treats, all priced cheaply. But parents like me know this can be deceptive, as once the children start choosing, they can ramp the cost up right high. Most children leave Whitford's carrying a brown paper bag of confectionaries and wearing a broad smile, some with their mouths already open, ready to devour a treat. Our boys were on their way to do the same.

Earl runs up first and checks out the jars, and I know he will have a hard time resisting his favorite, peppermints. Earl struggles to stray from the steady and reliable, where Bert will always go for something new and unknown. Mr. Whitford asks Earl if he wants his usual, which indeed he does, while Bert is pining for some of the new flavors of gum drops. Mr. Whitford takes a few of each of the candies, and drops them into the crisp brown bags, then hands them to the eager boys.

"Would you like anything else, Mrs. Reynolds?" He asks me.

"Could I please have a few pieces of chocolate for Mary Alice?" I always fret about her choking, as I know of a woman in the town who lost a child this way. There is no need to tempt fate with our littlest child, so the softer chocolate candy will be for Mary Alice.

Once each child has their own crinkled brown bag clutched tightly in their chubby little hands, Gibby asks about seeds for the farm. He saves what he can from his own stock, but he likes to see what new seeds are on offer. He is always looking for heartier, easier-growing plants.

"Nothing new for seeds, Gibby. I believe you have already purchased some of everything I had in stock," replies Mr. Whitford.

After thanking him, Gibby and I wander over to the spices, and I gather what I need for meals this week. I remember to pick up some yeast to make bread, and we bring our items to the counter to pay for them. Mr. Whitford tallies our items on a sheet and hands it to Gibby. As Gibby counts out his money, Mr. Whitford wraps everything together in a package of brown paper. He secures the package with some twine and then hands it over to me, while Gibby hands him the payment. Mr. Whitford takes the money and then places a single wrapped gumdrop on the counter, knowing how much I enjoy them. I pick it up and put it in my pocket to enjoy later.

"Thank you for your kindness," I tell him.

He nods and smiles at me. "Thank you, Gibby and Mrs. Reynolds. And I hope all goes well with your lying in," he replies.

"Thank you kindly," I reply, and we walk out into the sunshine and down the steps toward Smokey and the waiting wagon.

We all wait for our turns to get into the wagon on the cobblestone in front of the store, and while we're waiting a man and woman walk up to us, the man tipping his hat to Gibby and me. Everett Culver and his wife Delphine have walked the short distance up the hill to their home. Delphine is my good friend, and I am pleased to see her.

"You are looking lovely today, Mercy. Are you well?" Delphine asks me.

"Good as I can be, Delphine, so close to lying in. I am happy that you'll be with me when my time comes," I reply to her.

"I most assuredly plan on it, Mercy," Delphine is one of the town's many midwives, and she's been with me for my lying in with the other children. It's helpful and reassuring to have an experienced midwife who is also a good friend.

"We're looking forward to visiting your home tomorrow after services," says Delphine.

"And we're looking forward to having you," I reply.

Delphine and her husband own a large white farmhouse at the end of Pine Hill. The home is a lovely sight during the summer months, with rose bushes blooming profusely, draping themselves over the neat fence that surrounds the property. She has shared some with me, and I hope there will one day be a lovely cascade of these flowers on my wall too. We chat for a while as the children play in the dusty street, with Gibby keeping a watchful eye for wagons and horses.

"We'll see you on the morrow," I say to the Culvers a few minutes later. Everett tips his hat and he and his wife continue on up the hill with their little girls in tow.

Gibby turns to me, helps me into the wagon, and hands Mary Alice up to me.

Once we are all back in our wagon, Gibby untethers Smokey from the hitching post, pats his velvety nose and climbs up to take his place on the bench seat near me. He clicks his tongue at the horse, and we take off for home.

We pass the Flying Owl Tavern on the way out of town, and I see a few horses tethered outside, waiting for their owners. It's not always a good sign to see horses there so soon in the day, as their owners are taking their refreshments quite early, and not all the town's residents can hold their spirits well. I am truly grateful Gibby has no interest in drinking generally, except to toast a holiday or the birth of our babes. This can't be said for some of the men in town, who imbibe their spirits and then show a different, not always benevolent side. As we pass, I look towards the door and see Ebenezer Jones walking out of the tavern toward his waiting horse. He stumbles a little, and it saddens me. Ebenezer is married to the local trollop Bertha and he's most likely drowning his sorrows in liquor. I know if I was married to her I might be doing just the same. As we roll past he raises his hand in greeting, and Gibby waves back.

We soon reach the Pine Hill intersection and turn left onto it, approaching the Great Wall.

The Great Wall runs along the side of Pine Hill and stands as testament to the work of a local mason named Henry Sayles. The wall is high, and borders a large field. It took Henry Sayles four years to build it, and it's become a local landmark in our little town. The term "Great Wall," is used often by townsfolk to give directions to others.

"Since Whitford's is all out, I'm going to check with Kenyon Supply to see what they have when I stop in to purchase fertilizer next week," Gibby tells me as he drives us home.

Kenyon Supply is another of the town's general stores. It doubles as a tavern and meeting place for various town committees. It's similar to Whitford's but it doesn't have fabric or a particularly extensive candy selection. But what it lacks in those items, it makes up for in farming supplies.

"Well, I hope you will find what you need when you go," I reply. A plentiful harvest will store in our cellar to feed our family through the long winter months. It's always important to have a good harvest, and it's discouraging when we don't get a good yield. When that happens all you can do is hope next year will be better. Hope is certainly very addictive.

After a little while, we reach the end of Cedar Swamp and turn down our road to Hell Hollow. Down the hill we go, until we see the familiar row of lilacs and the stone wall in front of our homestead. I am always grateful to people like Mrs. Gordon and my friend Delphine for sharing their flowers. It is an extravagance we can't always afford, so I am deeply appreciative of them. I have always felt all these little details make a house a true home.

Gibby stops our wagon near the barn, and the minute it rolls to a halt the twins jump down and are off and running. I am not so nimble or so energetic, and once we are all on the ground I take Mary Alice's hand and head into our home.

Gibby and the boys stay to give Smokey some oats and a little hay, and check to make sure he has water. They do the same for our cow, Bessie, and once they're both settled in, he'll close the barn door and join us in the house. Later he will return to put the animals into their stalls. There used to be many predators in the area, but due to the large bounties on offer, most of the wolves and coyotes have been taken care of, so it is relatively safe to keep our animals outside. Even so, we sleep sounder knowing they are safe in their stalls.

As I enter our kitchen with Mary Alice I remember that we're low on fresh water, so I grab our large water jug along with Mary Alice and walk back outside to where Gibby is finishing with the animals.

"We need water. Would you like to join me for a walk to the spring?" I ask him.

"I was planning on taking the twins for a walk, so that sounds right fine," Gibby replies.

We have a small well at our home, but it's much easier to get water from a spring a short walk away from our home rather than bring up bucket after bucket from our well. The bonus is that the walk to the natural spring tires the twins out. I don't mind the exercise, as the movement will hopefully make my time easier when I deliver the baby. Gibby takes the jug from me, calls out to the twins, and we set off on our walk.

We stroll from our yard, and cross the road to a tree-lined path that leads directly to the spring, and arrive in good time. The spring itself is a unique sight, and always comes as a surprise. There's no sign of water anywhere, and then you suddenly come upon a clear pool bubbling from the ground, and a stream flowing from it down through the woods. I imagine the Native Americans who used to live here enjoying the spring in the same way we do, as an important source of water.

Gibby leans over the clear pool and dips our jug into it, letting the fresh water flow inside. The twins drop down beside him and scoop water with their hands, bringing it to their mouths to drink. The jug filled, Gibby sets it down, and he and I watch as the boys, now over the excitement of a fresh drink, run about in the field above the spring. Before long Bert gets too rambunctious and starts to wrestle with Earl. Earl is typically no match for his stronger brother, and it does not always end well, so I yell out that we have to return home, breaking the peaceful moment.

My timing is perfect, and heads off any injury to either boy. We start our walk home, the boys with less of a spring in their step, having spent their energy in the field. I've got a smile on my face because neither of them has a black eye, and neither of them is crying from some injury or other.

Back at the house, Gibby places the pitcher in our ice box, starts a fire in the cook stove, and heads to the parlor, while I take some potatoes and carrots from my little cupboard, cut them into smaller pieces, and add water to cook in the pot alongside some ham. Leaving this to simmer, I join my family in the parlor.

I sit down in my chair beside my husband, place my feet on my little stool, and enjoy the warmth from the fire Gibby has started. I tip my head back against the chair, thinking I will just rest my eyes for a moment.

Later, I feel someone touching my arm. It's Earl.

"Is dinner ready yet, Mama?" he asks quietly.

I realize with a start I have been sleeping for a while as a glance outside shows that the sun is setting in bright orange streaks across the sky, like hell is on fire outside my window.

"I'll go and check on it, little Earl," I reply, getting to my feet slowly and walking to my kitchen. As I stir the soup I can feel the vegetables have softened, and there is a nice broth as well. It looks like dinner is ready for my hungry family. Supper has been dutifully cooking itself while I was napping.

I set the table with utensils and bowls for the soup as Gibby comes into the kitchen with the children following like ducks in a row. We sit in our usual places, and I ladle soup into everyone's bowls, filling my own last. There is no sound in the room except for the tinkle of spoons as they tap the bowls while everyone eats.

"The Culvers will be visiting us tomorrow after church," I remind my family. Their faces light up as it is always a good day when other children come round to play.

"Perhaps you and Earl should get to bed early tonight so you can be up in time for services tomorrow. We don't want to be late in the morning," I tell the boys.

"Yes Ma'am," they reply in unison, as they scrape the last of their soup from their bowls.

With a full belly, Gibby retreats to the parlor, while the boys and I clean up the table and the kitchen. Our task does not take us long, and the boys soon run off to join their father and Mary Alice. I tidy up a few more things, then take the dirty water from washing to the back door to empty. I replace the bucket in its usual spot in the kitchen and then join them as well.

Some evenings, if I am not too tired, I will read one of the few books they have to them, the storylines taking the children to foreign lands or teaching them their letters. But it's been a very busy day and tonight was not one of those nights.

Entering the parlor I see Gibby has lit our kerosene lamp which casts the parlor in a warm, golden glow. He stoops over to stoke the fire, which fills the room with heat. I sit in my chair on the side of my husband's and put my feet up on my little stool. Gibby sits in his chair and looks over at me and we smile at each other. I put my head back on my chair and rest my eyes.

I slowly open my eyes to a much darker and silent parlor. I fell asleep again! Oh my goodness, what time is it? I rise to my feet and listen to the sounds of my children in their room. From the doorway I see Gibby is on the floor while the children clambering all over him.

Their bedroom consists of a full-size bed that the twins share and a smaller bed along the wall for Mary Alice. There is a small trunk at the foot of the twins' bed, a bureau for their clothes and a small toy chest.

Although many families have the children sleeping in the same bed, we make sure they have a bed of their own. This arrangement assures the twins do not kick and keep Mary Alice awake all night. It's never a pleasant day for anyone if the children wake up tired, and I try hard to avoid this. The twins like sharing a bed, but Mary Alice seems to prefer some room to herself. It works well, most of the time.

"Perhaps we should be settling down for sleep," I tell them all, as the children roll off their father, laughing.

Gibby turns to me saying, "Mama says it's time for bed."

The twins are well aware of their bedtime ritual, and they run for the water jug in the kitchen. I hear their footsteps as they return, with Bert appearing first in the doorway, carrying the water jug. It is a different water jug than the one we got this afternoon. It's a jug that stays on the shelf at room temperature, to be used for washing. Room temperature is much better than a pitcher that has been sitting in an ice box. Unless of course, it is a hot summer day.

Gibby collects the jug from Bert and pours a little water into the smaller pitcher on the bureau. To prepare the children for bed we take a damp washcloth, wet it from the pitcher and wipe their little faces and bodies, so they will sleep refreshed and clean. The twins get into their nightclothes, and Gibby helps Mary Alice with hers. While they are getting dressed for bed, I go to the trunk at the foot of the bed to get extra blankets. It is still cool in our house at night, and I want to make sure they are all nice and warm in their beds.

By this time the twins are more than ready to fall into bed, exhausted from running circles around each other all day, and Mary

Alice quickly follows suit. I look at Earl and Bert who are tucked up tight in their bed, the blanket to their chins, with their little heads peeking out waiting for a good night kiss. Gibby and I oblige, then kiss Mary Alice, who is also tucked like a bug in a rug in her own bed.

We blow out the lantern in their room and retreat to the parlor to repose. Gibby picks up his pipe, and I pick up my new book, *Little Women*, by Louisa May Alcott. I treasure reading a good book. Books have endless possibilities. They teach me things I did not know, they entertain me, and they take me to places I would otherwise never go.

Gibby is happy to just sit silently and relax most evenings, occasionally letting out a deep breath that's almost a snore. The only change is my book, and after a time I feel my eyelids getting heavy, so I put it down on the little table by my chair and awaken Gibby from his slumber. He blows out our lantern and then we walk to our bed together for a much needed sleep.

Sunday, May 6th, 1883

I wake up first, turn onto my side and slowly get out of bed. Being near the end of my time, I need to relieve myself often and I am thankful for the closeness of the chamber pot. I pull my pot out from under our bed and lift my nightgown. What a convenience it is to not have to run out in the cold to the privy every morning. After I finish, I slide the pot back under the bed, as I would like to get dressed before I go out into the cold yard to empty it.

Straightening up, I pull my finest dress out of my wardrobe, as today we are going to church. The dress is lilac in color, with lace detail at the sleeves and neckline. It is very ladylike, and I love to wear it. I've let it out and when I've had the baby I'll have to adjust it again if I want to keep wearing it. For now, I put on the everyday dress and a pair of some thick socks, and walk into the kitchen where I start breakfast for my family.

After a hearty breakfast of bacon, johnny cakes and fresh milk, we dress in our finest clothes to attend church. I help the children first, and the twins look truly handsome in their trousers and white linen shirts, while Mary Alice wears a little dress, all of which I sewed myself. Gibby wears a crisp pair of trousers, with a white shirt and a jacket. For church, he wears his bowler hat as well.

Dressed in my lilac dress with lace details, I grab my bonnet from the wardrobe. Seeing the bonnet gives me an idea, and I walk through our home and out our front door, heading over to our lilac shrub. I fasten a few sprigs of lilac to my hat with pins, and it matches my dress nicely.

Looking at my reflection in the mirror, I see green eyes, a round face and brown hair pulled back into my normal bun, and I hope I look as lovely as the lilacs do on my hat. The fragrance around me is wonderful, and it puts a smile on my face as I hasten back to my little family that waits so patiently for me. I look at them, all dressed in their best clothes and wearing cheeky smiles, and my heart swells. I take Mary Alice's hand and together we walk out through the back door to our wagon, where Gibby is waiting for us.

On the relatively short ride I listen to the birds singing and the steady rhythm of Smokey's hooves as he pulls us along the country road. I glance back into the wagon, where the twins are sitting nicely along the front, looking about themselves and also enjoying the bright sunshine. They probably hope that the service won't last long. It's a struggle for them to sit and listen these days, in the quiet church.

We arrive at the same time as many of the other parishioners, and we all look for a place to park our wagons. Gibby guides Smokey into a spot near the back, and positions him so we can just drive out when the service is over. He goes through the usual unloading routine, helping the twins down, then Mary Alice, and then me. I take Mary Alice's hand again as we walk toward the small Congregational Church sitting at the side of a field. It is a pretty church, with a steeple on its roof and a small number of steps leading up to a matching pair of large front doors. On this sunny day, the doors are open wide, and the church is inviting, welcoming us inside.

As a family, we walk together up the gray stone steps, through the wide-open doors and into the sanctuary of the church, with light streaming through the windows. I look around the open room and find us a pew towards the back. We all shuffle into the pew to sit, with Mary Alice sitting on my lap. I prefer seating our family at the rear of the Church, as many other families with young children do, because if the twins start fidgeting there won't be so many witnesses. Most of the time we are in good company with the other restless families. We can share an unspoken experience without attracting frowns from the older members of the congregation. As we sit, we watch the latecomers find seats, mostly in the front, and settle into their pews.

Once everyone is seated, Pastor Carpenter walks down the aisle, and goes straight to his pulpit. The Pastor is a kindly man, balding, with the remnants of brown hair. He has a round face, a mustache and kind eyes.

I try to relax on the hard and uncomfortable pew with my enlarged belly, surrounded by my fidgeting children, and pray the Pastor is merciful and it is a short sermon this week. I can feel my unborn child pressing on my bladder again.

"Good morning everyone." the Pastor smiles, and we answer him, wishing him a good morning as well.

"Today's sermon is about loving thy neighbor. The Lord says this is something we must do, but it is not always an easy thing to do." I smile at this statement, because it's easy enough for me with neighbors like the O'Dowds. But not everyone is as fortunate as me. I think again about Bertha Jones and I'm grateful she lives in the center of town, and not out here beside us.

"Good deeds tend to be quickly forgotten, but if someone is wronged no one forgets. Let us work on forgiving more, and loving more."

The sermon continues in this vein, and while the Pastor speaks I glance around at the congregation and see some people who really ought to be listening intently to the pastor's words. One can only hope! My twins are listening as well, but I know that will only last a short time, so I start to pray again that Pastor Carpenter keeps it short. The baby kicks and I wince.

But God must be listening on this lovely day, as the sermon is over before I know it, and lo and behold, the tithing man standing at the rear of the church has not tapped the shoulder or head of anyone in my family.

The tithing man keeps an eye on the parishioners, and if anyone is seen nodding off during the sermon, it is his duty to wake the dozing parishioner with his tithing stick. The tithing stick has a fox's paw on one end and its tail on the other. Little did the sorry fox know that his afterlife would be spent in the hands of an old fussbudget waking exhausted and bored parishioners in our little church.

To my dismay, Gibby has been prodded many a time by the little foot, and so has Bert. While adults appreciate a sermon, the children usually do not. And the longer the sermon goes on, the more restless the congregation gets. Especially my boys.

The tithing man does not tap ladies with the paw, instead he whisks the tail in the face of any woman who happens to take a midday rest during their time in church. This is always a possibility, as many of us are awake most evenings with a newborn or sick child, or just exhausted from pregnancy and the many chores we have to do to run our households. I am proud to say that I have never befallen the tithing stick's touch, even in my many states of pregnancy.

Thankfully my entire family evades the fox paw during this shorter than usual sermon. Perhaps the pastor knows that the sunny day is welcomed by all after another long, hard winter, and since it is the Sabbath, his parishioners are anxious to get about their day. We enjoy our weekly day of rest, what with all the things we need to do as part of our everyday lives.

When the service is over, we wait our turn with the rest of the churchgoers to file out of the church. Pastor Carpenter stands just outside the church doors to shake his parishioner's hands, and we thank him for an inspiring service. We don't thank him for its brevity, but we're grateful enough to emerge onto the smooth stone steps and out into the warm sun, where we see the Culvers who are waiting for us on the church lawn.

"Good morning, Delphine and Everett," I say to the couple, offering them a broad smile.

Delphine is striking today in her gray Sunday dress with blue ribbon details. The dress has lots of ruffles and a gray bonnet that matches it. Her hair is naturally curly, but today it's pulled back in a chignon that matches the dignity of church on Sunday. She has lovely brown eyes that sparkle in the sun, and to match her bubbly personality, some of the curls have escaped the bonnet and fall delicately around her face. But what really lights up Delphine is her beautiful smile.

"Good morning to you both. We were waiting to see if our plans were still on for this afternoon," Delphine responds.

"They certainly are! You are welcome to follow us home," I tell her, and both of our families climb into our respective wagons.

The Culvers have been to our home more than a few times, and they follow us down the road and into our yard. We unload, and the children head into the parlor, trying their best not to be over-anxious to eat so they do not get scolded. The men retreat to sit in the parlor, where they are surrounded by the children, while Delphine and I head for the kitchen to get lunch started. With Aunt Babette's assistance, I am once again serving Royal Ham Sandwiches. The twins love these sandwiches, and I surely hope the Culvers do as well. I chose them for our meal today because we don't have enough utensils to share with another family. To entertain others I have to be creative, and Aunt Babette helps me often.

The miniature sandwiches are filled with boiled ham, eggs, best butter, and mustard all spread onto a slice of bread. I have the ingredients already, and all I have to do is assemble them with some bread I have baked. I'll do this with Delphine's help. Yesterday I made doughnuts from a recipe in Aunt Babette's cookbook, and we will have those for dessert. I am hoping it will be a tasty feast that we'll all enjoy.

Delphine and I work in tandem, removing the ingredients from my ice box and then quickly assembling the sandwiches. Once we're done, we stack them onto a plate so that everyone can help themselves. I take my doughnuts off the shelf, where I had them hidden away from the prying eyes of the children, and set them down alongside the sandwiches, on a plate of their own. The children will have to be watched to make sure they take a sandwich first, as the twins are likely to stack doughnuts on their plates and run.

While we are putting together this meal for our families, Delphine and I catch up on local news.

"Have you met the new school teacher yet?" Delphine asks me. She is referring to Corinna Grenier, who has started a new school on Sterling Hill Road.

"Not in person, no, but I hear she's the talk of the town. Do you know she's teaching French along with English in that new school of hers? And she has opened a library," I tell Delphine. I am an avid reader and am looking forward to meeting her and borrowing some books.

"She is a widow and quite friendly. I ran into her at Whitford's just the other day," Delphine replies.

"She's a brave woman to travel down from Canada to a small rural town like this one. Maybe she has relatives in this area," I wonder aloud to Delphine.

"I believe she is related to the Rainvilles and some people in Almyville. I sure hope they're supporting her," Delphine says.

Once the table is set and lunch is ready, Delphine goes to the parlor and tells everyone to come through to the kitchen. While she is doing that I set a vase full of lilacs in the center of the table to make it pretty. I had cut the flowers earlier this morning for a vase for my table, and I put a few more sprigs in a cup for Delphine. I'll give them to her later, before she leaves.

Earl and Bert run into the kitchen first, and when they see me they halt right quick and slow their pace to a walk. They can run their energy off later, Sunday or not. They are followed by a toddling Mary Alice and Amelia, who are close in age, and then Aurore, who is about a year younger than the twins. Once everyone is seated, Delphine and I join them, and we sit at our little table to enjoy our meal together. We join hands, and Gibby asks Everett to say a blessing over our meal. Once he's finished, everyone drops their hands and helps themselves to my sandwiches. The meal is devoured without much conversation, and before long everyone's plate is empty apart from a few crumbs. A good sign indeed.

After the meal, which everyone seems to have appreciated, the men take their leave from us and call the older children to head outside to the barn. After everything has been put back into order in my kitchen, Delphine and I retreat to the parlor, where we join the younger children who are already at play.

"I am right pleased it's warming up. The threat of diphtheria will lessen," Delphine tells me. It was often thought that the warm weather helped stop epidemics, or at least shorten them.

"Yes, I am thankful both our families have passed the winter with no loss," I say, agreeing with my friend.

"How have you been feeling?" Delphine inquires of me. Giving birth is not an easy task and women are usually very supportive of one another, each hoping the lying in goes quickly and favorably for the mother, and as painlessly as possible, resulting in a healthy baby and mother.

"Best as I can expect with three babies already to take care of," I reply. "I am thankful the twins are older, they'll be able to help a bit once the new babe is here"

"Yes, that will definitely be useful for you. Have you decided on a name yet?"

"If it's a boy we'll call him Charles, and if it is a girl we plan on Maud Ella. Ella is a tradition in my family."

I have an aunt named Martha Ella, and there are many other women in my family who bear that middle name as well. I love tradition and would like to keep this one moving forward.

"Maud Ella is a lovely name, and I especially like Ella," Delphine says.

"It will be comforting to me to have you at my lying in, along with Cora," I tell her. I don't know what I would do without her and Cora at my side.

"I surely plan on it, and I know all will be well," Delphine reassures me.

"Remember what a surprise your first one was," She says with a smile.

My first lying in resulted in the twins, and we had no idea another babe was coming after the first one. My labor was lengthy, and Bert was born rather small, but once Earl arrived we realized why. They'd both been sharing space in my womb! Thankfully, despite arriving in this world so tiny, they thrived and grew strong.

"A surprise indeed, but such a welcome one!" I agree, smiling at the memory of my boys being born, and the surprise of not one baby but two.

We talk about the dinner coming up in June at the Grange, and all the wonderful things our children have been accomplishing, and we are soon caught up in each other's lives.

"Delphine, I believe it's time for us to take our leave 'fore we outstay our welcome," Everett says in his deep voice as he enters the parlor to collect Delphine.

There's a hint of laughter in his tone. Everett is a man of few words, but he has a very dry sense of humor and has the habit of leaving you giggling with stitches in your side after something he has said.

Delphine and I rise from our chairs and move toward one another to embrace. I remember the canning jar of lilacs in my kitchen. I savor one more second of Delphine's hug and then release her.

"Wait one minute, Delphine. I have something for you." I take the lilacs from the counter and return to the parlor to give them to her, and she smiles in delight.

"Lilacs from the Reynolds homestead, how wonderful! Thank you, Mercy!" Delphine says.

"You are most welcome! Hopefully, the shrub we gave you will start to bloom soon, and you'll have some in your own yard directly!"

I lean in to give her one more embrace, and she embraces me in return before turning to leave our home with her little family.

There are surely some people that you are always very thankful to see leaving, but Delphine and her family are never those people. We follow the Culvers out our back door and into the yard and watch as they climb up into their wagon, with little Amelia looking quite sleepy in her mother's arms. I am sure she'll be fast asleep long before they arrive home.

Everett helps his family into their wagon, walks around to the driver's seat and climbs up. He picks up the reins and lightly lifts them, so they tap the horse's back. It is the sign the horse has been waiting for, and he pulls the wagon out onto Hell Hollow Road. Everett tips his hat to us, while Delphine smiles, her hands too full of a slumbering baby to wave. Aurore waves at us while we wave till they are out of sight. We retreat into our home as the sun starts to set, bathing the landscape in a warm glow, heralding the end of another day.

Tuesday, May 8th, 1883

Our fireplace in the parlor crackles with bright flames on this cool spring evening, creating a warm glow and bringing some welcome heat into our home. The children are at our feet, Gibby is contentedly smoking his pipe, and we are relaxing together after a day filled with chores and children's antics. There is peace and a comfortable silence when I feel my pains start. It may take a while or it may not, only the babe knows, but Gibby needs to get Delphine and Cora so they can attend my lying in. As calmly as possible I tell him my time has come, and he grabs his boots. Cora is closest, so he will go there first, and then onto Delphine's.

"Thank you, Gibby. I do believe you have some time, so don't you go rushing and make that poor horse ill," I tell him.

He hastens to me, kisses me on my cheek, and then turns to leave. Soon after I hear the rapid drumming of hoofbeats and know he is on his way.

I rise out from my chair to get the children ready for bed. The bedtime ritual progresses smoothly, as if they know they have to behave themselves tonight, and once they are settled I return to our room to make preparations for the birth.

Sitting in our bed wearing a single nightshirt, I am happy to hear the door open and close, and footsteps heading toward my room. Delphine flies in, breathless from hurrying, while Gibby stays outside tending to her horse. She is an expert horsewoman and easily rode back on her own horse to our home with Gibby. They got here quicker than Cora, but Gibby tells me he'd been to her house too.

"Mercy, how are you feeling?" Delphine inquires as she tries to catch her breath and remove her cloak at the same time.

"My pains are close together, but my water hasn't broken yet," I tell her.

"I think it best we get you walking. It'll help you to get your water to break," she says as she puts a bag on the floor and walks over to help me out of our bed. I clutch her arm and double over as pain grips my middle. I have been blessed with quick and easy births, and I hope my luck continues with this baby. I clutch her arm and pull myself up to pace the room with her.

"There's an old sheet at the end of the bed. Could you double it over so it will protect my bed when the baby comes?" I ask Delphine. She leaves my side and quickly folds the sheet in two and places it where I will be laboring. After the delivery, my nightshirt, linens, and sheets will be cleaned with baking soda, in the hope that we can salvage them. But in case they're spoiled beyond redemption, I try to use older items.

Gibby enters the room and asks if we need anything, and Delphine asks if he had told Cora.

He nods. "I went there first as she was closest, but something must have kept her. Or maybe Delphine just rides a whole lot faster." He smiles at Delphine, and I think how nice it is to have two women helping with a birth, as it is anyone's guess how it will go.

While we are waiting for Cora, Delphine and I pace in my room, my pains coming quickly, with very short intervals between them. Before we know it, Cora is at our side, as breathless as Delphine was earlier.

"Sorry I'm so late," Cora says as she takes off her cloak and places her belongings on the floor. "Frederick wasn't feeling well, and it was difficult to leave." She tells us.

"I understand, I'm just glad you were able to make it here at all," I tell Cora, with as much of a smile I can muster through the pain.

Cora is Irish, like her husband, with fair hair and skin and bright blue eyes. She has an Irish brogue, which I always enjoy listening to.

Delphine and I have been continually walking around my room, and my water finally breaks. The ladies wipe my legs with some clean rags I had collected for my lying in, and clear up what liquid there is on the floor, while I go to my bed, hoping it won't be much longer till the baby comes.

At least I hope it won't be.

Cora holds my hand and stays at my side, as Delphine sits at the end of my bed and looks between my legs to see how far along I am.

"You are looking well and close Mercy," she tells me.

"Thank the good Lord for it," I pant. Like any other birth, I want it over quickly, with the babe healthy. It's been a few hours since my labor started, and in time my pains get closer together and Delphine finally announces it's time for me to push.

Cora helps me sit against headboard of the bed so I can brace myself, and I begin the arduous task of pushing the baby out. My friends are coaxing me to push, and not stop pushing, but I'm getting exhausted from the hours of laboring. The room feels warm and sticky from the combined activity of the three of us and the glow from a few lanterns someone has lighted. My hair is damp at my neck from laboring, and I am getting worn out. After what feels like an eternity of pushing, I finally hear Delphine exclaim she sees the head.

"Thank heavens," I tell her.

"Just a few more pushes, Mercy!" Delphine says, and I grip Cora's hand. By the third babe, I knew to wait for the natural contraction of my body, and to add a push of my own as well. I do this a few times, with Cora and Delphine encouraging me, and at last I feel the release of the baby from my body.

"I have the babe!" Delphine excitedly says. I lie back on my pillow while Cora wipes my forehead with a cool cloth.

"You did well, Mercy, just like before," she says, as I close my eyes with exhaustion. I finally hear the squawk of a baby, and when I open my eyes, Delphine is holding a red-faced bundle to my breast.

"What is it?" I ask exhaustedly.

"She's a perfect little girl," Delphine answers. We are all crying tears of joy that it's over, and that it all went well. Delphine wraps the baby in a clean blanket, and places her back in my arms so I can get a good look at her. While Cora and I are examining the baby, Delphine delivers my afterbirth, which she puts into a used blanket, but not before she cuts the umbilical cord. I am so grateful it is over, and that both the babe and I are healthy.

"Welcome to the world, Maud Ella," I tell my new daughter.

Cora works around my bed, straightening it so that I'm comfortable. Delphine goes to Gibby to let him know it is over and that he has a new daughter.

I gaze into the perfect little round face of the baby I'm holding in my arms. She has a small tuft of blonde hair on the top of her head, and perfect pink skin with no wrinkles or markings. She opens her eyes once, and I see the dark orbs looking around for a moment, then she closes them as though the whole simple process was just too tiring. She may well be exhausted like me. What an ordeal they go through coming into this world. I place my finger near her cheek to see if she is hungry, as I am ready to feed her, but she does not root toward my finger, and seems instead to be content just to slumber.

While I am enjoying this moment, Gibby rushes into the room, with anxiety written all over his face. His forehead is shiny, as I am sure he's been perspiring with worry. He went many years without a family of his own, and now he has four healthy children. He doesn't say much, but when I see his face, I see so much love and happiness. He hastens to my side and looks down wide-eyed, taking in his new daughter.

"Meet your daughter, Maud Ella Reynolds," I say to my husband, whose eyes are bright with tears. He looks at me and gives me a huge smile. We are both relieved it is over, and all is well. His lips touch my cheek and then he sits at my side as we both gaze at our newest child.

Monday, June 4th, 1883

It has been a full month since Maud Ella was born. She is a lovely baby, easy-going and hardly causes a fuss. It's almost like she knows she's arrived into a large family and wants to be helpful by being easy-tempered. I am filled with such gratitude to have four healthy children, a home, and a husband who loves me. What blessings I have, when others have so little or have lost loved ones.

Our life is not always easy, with the hardships of farming, but I choose to look on the positive side. Without the difficult moments, we'd never appreciate the joyful ones. There is something to say for enjoying each moment life brings us, as life is so delicate and can be snuffed easily through disease, accidents, or simply age.

I try to hold onto memorable moments, such as the first time Mary Alice called me "Mama" or when the twins bring me flowers they discover in our yard clutched in their little hands, with identical big toothy smiles. It is hard sometimes not to worry over what might happen to my little family in these difficult times, but worrying only ruins the moment. My fears will hopefully never become reality, so I commit all these moments to memory, hoping there will be many more joyful moments to come.

While I have been busy with the new baby and my usual household chores, Gibby has finished planting, cutting firewood, and doing his usual tasks. Life is marching steadily forward and it's as full as ever. There is a gathering planned on Saturday at the new Grange, picnic-style, with music and most likely dancing, which I am looking forward to. This will be the first time Maud Ella has attended a social event, as well.

Delphine and Cora have visited me to check on the babe, and to see if I need anything. I am again filled with gratitude toward my friends. My belly has gone down considerably, and I am now taking a gown in so that it fits for the dance, as I would like to look my best for my first public appearance after my lying in. With my everyday chores and a new babe, there does not seem to be enough hours in the day to get everything done.

As well as finishing my dress, I will need to bring a meal for us to eat for dinner. As usual I will be referring to Aunt Babette's helpful cookbook. Seeing as how we will be traveling there in the wagon and eating picnic-style, I'm thinking I may make my Royal Ham Sandwiches again. They are a favorite, they will travel, and they'll be easy for us to eat.

After I decide on our picnic, I realize I am behind on cleaning Maud Ella's diapers. They need to be scraped clean, if needed, washed on the washboard, then boiled on my cook stove afterwards. It is a lengthy process and one I dread. But I perform the task while Maud Ella sleeps happily in her little basket near me. Since I am doing a wash, I wash some of our clothes as well. Once they are all clean, I walk out my back door to the clothesline which hangs from our home to a post across our yard. I hang all the diapers and clothes on the line to dry in the fresh air. As I clip them to the clothesline, the breeze fills them like sails, and they sway on the line. The sunny day and breeze will dry them in no time. Maud Ella is next to me again, in her little basket. The chores have taken me all afternoon and I am well and truly tired by the end of the day.

Saturday, June 9th, 1883

I am preparing my sandwiches early this morning, and making lemonade for the festivities today. Later this afternoon, we're attending a picnic with banjo playing at the Ekonk Grange.

The Grange is a new organization in town and is very supportive of local farmers. Our new Grange already has many members, and it is located in a newly constructed building on Ekonk Hill across from our church.

The Grange will hold fairs and contests to see who has the best produce, flowers and livestock, and its members will swap seeds and knowledge so that everyone can prosper. It is a fitting arrangement for us all, and we enjoy spending time with the other members.

It's mostly for farmers, so there aren't many mill workers or other tradesmen at our functions. Those people we see in church, in town, or as guests in our own homes. The Culvers are tradespeople, and not Grange members, so we won't be seeing them tonight. But Cora and Jasper are coming, and it will be nice to see them and talk farming. Most farmers in our area struggle, although not as much as us in Hell Hollow, and it is very generous of any farmer to share the things that work best for them.

We're all just trying to survive, and any help is always welcome. Of course, there are always some selfish people who only think about themselves, but some of the farmers will still share with them in the hope they will learn to be generous rather than inconsiderate folks. But who can say if they'll ever learn? Pastor Carpenter says we must pray for such people, which I do, but I have yet to see a few of these clods transform. Only the Lord knows if they ever shall.

I was able to alter my dress in time, which seems a minor miracle in itself, and Delphine gave me some leftover ribbon, of which I have added a little to my dress and my bonnet. I am hoping I will be a sight to make my husband proud.

The children are growing so fast, I can barely keep up with stitching their alterations and new clothes as well. Thankfully I have Mary Alice's old clothing, so Maud Ella is dressed well, but I'll be needing to make new clothes for all my children very soon. It will be getting warm as the season moves toward full summer, and they will need lighter clothing to be comfortable. A mother's work is never done!

The sampler I am making for our privy still sits by my parlor chair as it is more of a frivolity than a necessity.

The sun streams through the window in my kitchen, brightening the pages of my ever-helpful cookbook as I thumb through it. As I peruse it I pass notes of who likes what recipe, and what to add or prepare to make it better for our family. Sometimes the book seems more like a family a memoir. There are stories in there for anyone who cares to look.

I turn the cookbook over to its side to look for the folded page corner marking the recipe for our favorite Royal Ham Sandwiches. Once I find it I use it to open the book to that page. I shall soon know the recipe by heart because of how many times I make these delectable sandwiches, but it's good to refer to the book to make sure I am preparing them correctly.

Lemons are not a local fruit, and they aren't always easy to come by. But I have been lucky enough to find some, as I do enjoy lemonade. I will take the juice from the ones I have and add some sugar and water to make the refreshing drink. Another benefit of the lemonade is my kitchen smells so fresh! I make haste with my work, and before long my kitchen is clean and my home smells lovely.

Praise be to Aunt Babette for sharing all her recipes that make festivities and everyday life tastier!

My family is running around like chickens being chased by a fox, preparing themselves for this afternoon's get-together. The children are dressed in their normal play clothes, as they will be playing with the other children at the gathering, and Gibby is wearing his usual trousers and suspenders, while I am working hard at fitting into my altered dress that I seem to have taken in a bit too much.

Merciful heavens! Of all times to be incorrect with my sewing skills. I am just about to remove my dress when Gibby enters our bedroom and tells me I look right pretty. Well, I guess comfort will have to be forgotten, as I am not going to switch dresses now. My others are all a bit large, and I haven't had the time to alter them to my new size. Let's hope the material will give a bit as the days wears on. The dress is my favorite, gray in color with shortened sleeves, and lace details at the neckline and bodice. It has layers of ruffles which are impractical for everyday wear, and it's far too fancy for church, but I enjoy wearing it. I don't have many dresses like this one, because of the impracticality, so it's a treat to wear it!

I find my boots and lace them up. They are a bit worn, but I'm not worried as they hardly show under my long skirts. It's an added benefit of wearing lengthy skirts. With four babes, we can hardly afford extras, so I make do with my one pair of boots.

Maud Ella is in a basket in my room, quiet and content, probably because I've just fed her. I reckon she shall fall asleep soon, which will make the afternoon even more relaxing. I fed her before we leave as it isn't proper to feed a babe at your breast in mixed company. Sometimes there's an area for nursing mothers, off to the side, but like to be prepared just in case and arrive with a full and satisfied baby. I am hoping she'll stay that way for most of the afternoon. Time will soon tell.

I take one final look at my reflection in the mirror and adjust my hair. I am wearing it in a bun as I usually do, but some of it has escaped and is falling in wisps about my face. I pin them back into place and tie a pale blue ribbon around my bun. I pinch my cheeks to liven them with color, and once I'm happy with how I look, I head to the back of the house where everyone is waiting.

Gibby herds the three older children, whom I got ready earlier, out the rear door, and I follow with Maud Ella, who is wrapped tight inside a light blanket in my arms. I have brought some rags to change her bottom if need be, and a blanket as well for if the afternoon turns cool. I try hard to be prepared always, but it seems some days I never am. I am as always, a work in progress.

I hand Maud Ella off to my husband and pull myself onto our wagon. Once I'm settled in my seat, I turn to glance at our older children, who are all sitting nicely against the back of the bench, anxious to get going. Gibby passes Maud Ella to me. She is still surprisingly alert, and I clutch her close to me. Gibby walks round to his side, hauls himself up, flicks Smokey's reins and we are on our way, out of our yard and up the hill out of Hell Hollow.

We arrive at the Grange along with many other farmers, and seeing the activity gets the children excited. They are bouncing about in the wagon, anxious to get down, and we wave at other families as we pass. Gibby eventually finds a spot in the back, and we stop and unload our family and picnic food.

Everyone plays their part by carrying something from the wagon, and we start walking toward the Grange building, stopping occasionally to say hello to people we meet on the way. It is such a lovely summer day, and the townsfolk are all enjoying the bright sunshine. After a dismal winter, you truly appreciate days like this.

We reach the rear of the building and look for a place to spread our blanket. Since the Grange is all new, there still aren't enough chairs to seat all the members and their families, which is why this jamboree is a less formal picnic style.

There are quite a few members and families sprawled out in the sunshine enjoying their food, and once we settle in, we do the same. We are just starting to eat our sandwiches when I see the O'Dowds. I wave to them, and they head over to us, with intentions of sitting beside us. The twins are as thrilled as a bear finding honey, as they do so love the O'Dowd boys.

Cora and Jasper spread out their blanket next to ours and start unpacking their own picnic. Our boys desert us to sit with the O'Dowds' sons. I know soon enough that all four of them will be off the blanket and heading off to visit other children. It is a wonderful thing to have these get-togethers, as life can be lonely for children on farms.

Cora is seated near me, while Gibby and Jasper are also seated near one another, discussing farming.

"How are you finding the Wylie School for Samuel?" I ask Cora. I am hoping to send the two boys to school in the fall. They're five years old, and ready to start their education. They get restless at home now, and they need something to stretch their minds.

"Mr. Wood is a wonderful teacher. He's very patient with Samuel and the others. I am pleasantly happy with the school so far," She informs me.

The Wylie School is not very far from where we are. It's a one-room school, and one of many schools within our town. The benefit of having quite a few schools is we do not have to travel far to take our children there. When the children are a bit older, they will walk to school by themselves.

Since we are neighbors with the O'Dowds, we will most likely share taking the boys back and forth to school. The Wylie School teacher, Mr. Wood, is known to be one of the better teachers in our town. He seems kind as well as knowledgeable, and I am grateful his is the school closest to us.

"I plan on sending Bert and Earl to the Wylie School as well this fall. Do you want to share the task of taking them there and back?" I ask her.

"That sounds wonderful, Mercy! School starts promptly at nine am and is over at one. We'll talk about it more nearer the time," she says.

"There was a lot of sickness last winter year, and we kept Frederick home often, much to his dismay," Cora tells me. Frederick is very studious and enjoys school, and I am hoping my boys will be the same. A good teacher makes attending school more enjoyable, and the kids don't dread it the same way they would cleaning manure off their boots.

"I am sorry to hear about the illness at school. It's been a hard year all around. I hope when the twins start school it'll be easier for them," I say to her.

"I agree, Mercy," Cora replies. She stares at what I am drinking. "Is that Aunt Babette's lemonade?" she asks me.

"It most certainly is, and I have some extra for you and Jasper," I take out two extra glasses I have brought and pour out some of the liquid into them. The glasses frost as I pour the liquid, which is still cold and quite refreshing.

Cora takes a glass and hands the other to her husband, who smiles at both of us. We all raise our glasses in salute, and take a refreshing sip, enjoying each other's company, the lovely day and the fact that our children are happy and content.

After a few moments of relaxation and more idle talk, Cora starts to pick up from dinner, which she and her family have finished, and I do the same. There is to be a hay ride after supper, something we're all looking forward to.

Once the remnants of our meals have been cleared away, the men return our picnic baskets to our respective wagons. We keep our blankets where they are on the ground in case we need somewhere to sit during the afternoon.

There is a commotion as Charlie Rounds arrives. He has a team of horses pulling a large wagon, and they look very fine in all their tack. They are draft horses, pale blonde in color, with white hair at their hooves. Charlie stops the wagon, and the team of horses stomp their feet and shake their heads, their manes flowing and waving at the movement. They are a glorious sight. I have always enjoyed the beauty of a well-tended team of horses, especially the larger draft horses with their huge hooves and hair flaring out like wings at their feet.

I have seen horses that haven't been taken care of, and it's a depressing sight, so to see these healthy and well-maintained animals is uplifting. Gibby always says you can tell a person's character by the state of their animals.

Charlie is a kind man, and as well as taking such great care of his animals he also runs the only cider mill in our town. In the fall he presses apples there, and we can purchase apple cider, hard cider, and even vinegar from him. It is his main source of income, but given that he is the proprietor of the only cider mill in town, it tends to be profitable. He has become quite prosperous from his cider and by-products, and he's generous to others who aren't so fortunate.

Gibby will sometimes work at his apple orchard in the fall to make additional coin, and it has the added benefit of fresh apples for us as well.

Charlie and his beautiful team of horses draws a crowd to see the magnificent beasts up close. When we arrived earlier, we were told he'd be offering hay rides through the fields behind the grange, and the children are gathering in a throng around his wagon

We and the O'Dowds are lucky to be some of the first people to get on board, and the boys are happy we can all ride together. There are haybales for seats along the sides of the large wagon, and the middle is open so that the youngsters can sit safely. Once we are settled in on the hay, Charlie calls to the horses to start them on their way.

The wagon pulls away smoothly, and I sit back to enjoy the ride. We travel around the edges of the field, where the crops are growing and doing well. We pass a new home being built and smell the magnificent scent of freshly cut wood. There are older farmsteads too, already up and running. The Dow homestead is one of these established homes, and it's a farm like the others. The Dows' son left the area and now lives in New York City where he runs a business with his partner called the Dow Jones Company. He is currently working as a journalist writing about the stock market, and he's started to make quite a name for himself. His family is quite proud of him, and rightly so. Some people leave their little towns like ours and go on to do great things like Charles Dow, but most of us, like myself, never leave.

I wonder about this as we pass the Dow family farm. What gives someone the courage to move on? It must be a very brave person to believe in themselves so much. Of course, a bit of coin helps as well. I have a lot of respect for those who venture out from their secure little part of the world and into the unknown. I hope the young Dow continues to make his mark in the world and inspires others. Maybe he will even inspire one of my brood.

We are now on the return trip of our ride, which has been great fun. The Grange building comes into view, and the wagon stops near the entrance while we wait our turn to disembark. When it's our turn, Gibby jumps down and helps the rest of us from the wagon. We see some other farmers and stop to chat. Gibby talks farming with some of the other men, and we women talk of our babes while the children run in circles about us.

It is a delightful afternoon, and everyone is in good spirits and looking forward to a prosperous harvest. Our conversations have slowly returned us to our blanket, and Gibby picks it up and folds it. Although disappointed, the twins help him, while I wait holding Maud Ella, with Mary Alice near my skirts.

Then, all at once it seems, the day is over, and we are heading home along with many others. Our timing is impeccable, as the sun is starting to disappear behind the trees, making a lovely sight. We are blanketed in the soft golden glow as the shadows of the trees stretch out across the fields, impossibly long in the evening light, and we enjoy the last moments of the warm sun on our skin. Even Smokey has a golden hue to his coat, and his gait is a bit quicker as he is impatient to get back to his stall and the oats that Gibby will give him as soon as we get home. The setting sun's lovely glow accompanies us all the way to Hell Hollow, making our travels smooth and safe.

When we reach our home, Gibby drops us off at the house, then heads to the barn to feed the animals and put them up for the night.

Once inside the house, I help the children get washed and ready for bed. When they're clean again, we all retire to our usual spots in the parlor with the children quietly playing at our feet.

The wonderful benefit of days like today is that the children are typically worn out, and more receptive to the idea of retiring into their beds.

The parlor glows from the lanterns I've lit around the room, extending our shadows along the walls, making the room seem cozy. Reclining in our parlor chairs, with our feet on little stools, Gibby speaks, breaking the tranquil moment.

"Mr. Lamoureux is thinking about selling his farmstead. He has not had a good season in a while, and he's struggling to pay his bills," he informs me.

"What does he plan to do?" I ask my husband, truly wondering, as this may be our future as well. There are a lot of local farmers like us, struggling to make ends meet.

Farmers enjoy being their own employer, but it's an uneasy arrangement, as nothing is guaranteed. A rainy season, swarms of pests, or just bad luck with seeds can make a pitiful harvest, and a bad year that hardly yields enough for our family will not provide enough left over to sell for profit. This was why it was so discouraging when we have a poor harvest.

We always hope that next year will be better. It is a precarious arrangement, but if I'm honest, I guess most ways of making a living are precarious these days. I wonder if this is how it will always be for us and our children. A mill worker toils running a machine all day under a miserable boss with the threat of firing each day, but a shopkeeper depends on people having enough money to spend on necessities, never mind extravagances. Nothing is easy it seems.

"I believe he may apply at the Sterling Mill," Gibby replies sadly. I know he is morose, possibly even considering his own eventual fate, as at any moment he may be doing the same thing. The mantel clock ticks on, emphasizing the silence as we sit together, lost in our own thoughts.

Soon the clock strikes eight o'clock, and I rise from my comfortable chair to gather the children for bed. As I leave the room, I look back to see Gibby contemplative, the smoke from his pipe making him appear lost in a fog. Which he may well be, so lost in thought he is.

Sunday, July 15th, 1883

I wake with a start as the smell of smoke fills my nose. Daylight fills the room, and I am grateful there is no smoke indoors at least.

"Gibby, do you smell that?" I nudge him.

He must get a whiff of smoke as he wakes quickly, sits up and starts pulling on his pants. The smoke seems to be even thicker now that we are aware and awake.

A fire is a terrible fear for any homesteader. Most buildings are made of wood, which means there's not a lot of hope for any structure once a blaze breaks out, and everyone tries to be very careful to avoid the possibility of a fire. It is even more dangerous in the summer when everything is dry, like it is now.

We both dress hastily, and immediately check on our children, sighing with relief when we find them fast asleep in their beds. Checking the rest of our home, we are relieved again that nothing's on fire, but our next thought is of where the smoke is coming from.

"I'm going to take Smokey out to see if I can find the source. I might be able to help," Gibby tells me, pulling on his boots. I watch as he runs to the barn to saddle Smokey, and then quickly takes off up the road. By now the sky is gray with smoke, and I know that wherever the fire is, it isn't far.

The children soon wake, and we eat breakfast and stay inside while we wait for news. Gibby has been gone a few hours and I am filled with worry. Fighting a fire is not an easy task – in fact, many times the most that can be done is to watch the structure burn, and hope everyone got out safely. I say a small prayer hoping that wherever the fire is, no souls are harmed.

Sitting in the parlor with the children at my feet, I hear a knock on my back door which startles me. I hasten to the window to see who is calling, and then open the door to Cora and her boys.

"Hello Cora, have you heard any news?" I ask her. She must be aware of the fire, as Jasper is not with her, and the smoke has filled all the hollow. The air is full of dust and smoke and small fragments of unidentified charred things that blow on the wind. Wood, paper, straw, the charred remnants of someone's livelihood. I check our roof again. If anything lands up there that is still burning, the results could be catastrophic.

"No news as of yet. Jasper left early this morning as soon as we noticed the smoke. I am tired of being alone and fretting about everything, so I thought I would stop by so we could pass the time together." I open the door wider, and she comes in with her boys.

We all return to my parlor to pass the time, hoping we'll hear some news soon. The children can sense the stress, and the smell of smoke is heavy as well.

A few hours pass and we finally hear the sound of a horse arriving in the yard. I run outside to see who has arrived, and thankfully it is Gibby. I follow him to our barn, where he dismounts and starts to unsaddle Smokey.

"Thank the good Lord you're safely home. Where was the fire?" I ask my husband.

"Up at the Pendleton farmstead on Ekonk hill, just downwind of the Dow farm," he tells me as he takes Smokey's bridle off. This explains why the smell of smoke was so heavy, as the fire was close by.

"Mrs. Pendleton was cooking and started a grease fire. It quickly got out of Hand, and before she could get help, the whole kitchen went up," Gibby tells me this as he brushes Smokey.

I know that once a good part of the home is aflame, there is not much hope for the rest of it.

"I stayed for a while helping out the fire brigade as they worked so no other buildings went up too. The Pendletons had a large barn close by, and we wanted to try to save their livestock, at least. The animals were panicked, what with the fire so close, and people were trying to calm them, as well as make sure the fire did not catch in the barn." Gibby leads Smokey to his stall and lets him in, closing the door behind the horse. He adds some grain to his bucket, then turns to me and I wait for him to speak.

"The house is gone. The Pendletons are staying with some family nearby, and we'll see what if anything can be salvaged from the home." Gibby tells me.

A kitchen fire is always a worry, as a fire can travel quickly. This is a case in point, and I feel for poor Mrs. Pendleton, cooking for her family and then unintentionally burning their home to the ground. Sadly fires are pretty common, and dry conditions and distance can make a large difference in containing a fire. Someone has to tell the fire brigade, get to the station, and then travel back to the fire. This takes time, and the further from town you are, the higher the chances will be that it'll all be just too late.

"Has everyone been accounted for?" I ask him, because although the loss of a home is terrible, the loss of a loved one is so much worse.

"All souls are safe, thank the Lord. Once everything settles, we'll all get out there and help them rebuild," Gibby tells me.

That is the nice thing about these rural towns. People helping each other in times of need.

Gibby closes the barn doors, and we walk to our home together to tell Cora the sad news.

Wednesday, August 1st, 1883

It's been a very long, hot and dry summer. Gibby has worried about the lack of rain, and our crops are struggling. But despite everything, it somehow looks like we will have a good yield. I do believe all the farmers in our area will be thankful when this stressful season is over.

I've started sewing quilts in the evening to try to make up for any shortfall we may have. I spend most summer evenings bent over my sewing and have two quilts almost ready for sale, which is fortuitous timing with fall arriving, and winter to follow. I am hopeful other people will be needing a warm quilt, and their need will provide our family with necessary coin.

Mr. Whitford has kindly allowed me to display a quilt in his store when it's finished, and I hope it will sell quickly and maybe attract a few orders for more.

As well as the quilt I plan to sell, I am making one for the Pendletons. They lost pretty much everything in the fire, and I feel for them so. They'll need a warm quilt once they are back in a home of their own.

The town has gotten together to help them rebuild, just like we thought they would. Lumber has been donated, and men have given their time. I am proud of our little town and how we take care of our own. Gibby and Jasper have spent many summer evenings helping the Pendletons rebuild their home, and it is coming along nicely.

The menfolk are working hard to get the family back indoors before winter arrives, and the womenfolk are helping in our own way as well. Any extra household items or clothing we can spare, we do, and I believe the Pendletons will be in a new home before long, and we are proud to help put them there.

Tuesday, August 7th, 1883

The twins are excited to be starting school soon, and I am enjoying their excitement as well. It's wonderful to see them practicing their letters on their little slates and looking forward to going. They will be attending to the school nearest to us, which is the Wylie School House, with Mr. Wood as a teacher.

The back door slams, and Gibby comes in with the twins, asking if I am ready to leave. We have plans to call on Jasper and Cora this afternoon.

"Yes, I am ready," I reply, placing the quilt down beside my chair in its basket.

Mary Alice moves her blocks to the side, and Gibby picks Maud Ella up from where she was lying. Both of my girls are so easy. They hardly ever cause a fuss and are beloved by all.

The twins are becoming Gibby's little shadows. Farms like ours need all the help we can get, so children are included in chores as soon as they are old enough to be.

"Mary Alice, could you please place those blocks in their sack so we can bring them along with us?" I ask my older daughter.

"Yes Mama," she answers.

I pass Gibby, who is still holding Maud Ella. She is smiling, and I smile at her in return.

"I'll fetch the picnic basket and then will be ready," I tell him.

"Let's go, Mary Alice," Gibby says, and she takes the sack of blocks and follows her father out the back door to Smokey and our waiting wagon. I hasten to the kitchen to grab the biscuits and cookies I made earlier and place them into the picnic basket. I add a few other items we'll be needing and head out the back door that the rest of my family passed through a few seconds before. I walk to the wagon and hand my basket up to Gibby, who places it carefully on the seat beside him.

We start out of our yard and turn right, instead of our usual left, and roll downhill into the hollow.

Our friends are further down the road, past the pond and Mrs. Clara Gordon's home. We pass Mrs. Gordon's pretty little house, but we don't see her. She is usually outside at this time of year, working on her immense gardens. She is a wonderful gardener, and has a stunning display of flowers as well as a variety of herbs for cooking and medicine.

Because she dabbles in medicinal herbs, some of the residents of our town are a bit afraid of her. She got very upset with some boys who stole blooming lilacs from her a few years ago and cursed them, so she now has a bit of a reputation in our little town, although we don't go as far as to use the word "witch". Thankfully, I have had nothing but kind interactions with her.

Clara was born into a wealthy family and had traveled throughout our country and even parts of Europe before she settled in the hollow with her husband. In fact, she had met her husband on one of these trips, but sadly she wasn't long married before he passed. Between her family's wealth and his success as a salesman, she was left well off.

Sadly, people have tried to take advantage of her, so she has become a little bitter over the years, in addition to the sorrow of losing her husband. She now lives alone, with a niece that visits once in a while from the South.

I think she's had a tough life, despite all the travelling and wealth, and I always try to be patient with her. One thing's for sure, I haven't walked in her boots, so I always give her the benefit of the doubt.

I try to stop by when I can, but my family keeps me busy most days, and it is not always easy to stop in for a visit. Knowing she can be a bit crotchety, I would rather visit alone and without the twins. They could test the patience of a saint somedays, so I wouldn't want to take a chance of Mrs. Gordon disliking my boys. We are on great terms with her, and I'd like to keep it that way – if only to avoid the chance of being cursed.

She is a great resource for cooking herbs, and has passed some of them on to me to grow. I have planted a little garden outside my back door, in a great spot, as it is not far from my kitchen. Many times I have been cooking and then run outside for a sprig of thyme, parsley, or garlic so the garden location is truly convenient.

I have planted lavender in this little garden as well, and the scent travels into our home on some summer days which is much more welcome than the ripe smell of the privy, which also invades our home if the wind is right.

We pull into the O'Dowd's yard and see their homestead, a rectangular house with a porch and a small extension off one side. Many of us have similar homes, as this style is quite economical to build and also popular at the moment.

Their homestead sits in the middle of a few fields, and they have a few more outbuildings than we do, as well as a much larger barn for livestock. Almost all of their land has been cleared for their fields, so their land is wide open, with one single tree near their home. This tree is large and provides a nice amount of shade to give them a bit of respite during hot summer days. Jasper has also hung two ropes, attached to a board from a branch, so they have a nice swing for the children to play on as well. My boys love this swing, and I always think I need to get Gibby to make one for our home as well. Theirs is a pretty home, with lots of nice wood details, the large tree shading it, and flowers blooming in the flowerbeds outside.

Cora and Jasper have struggled this season, and they haven't been as lucky as us with their crops. I only hope they have enough of a harvest to keep them going, as I do not know if they supplement with selling quilts and firewood like we do. I do know the latter is impossible as their land has been cleared of trees, so I only hope they have some other means of revenue, as I enjoy having them as neighbors.

Gibby brings the wagon to a standstill, and is waiting patiently at my side for me to hand him Maud Ella so I can climb down. Once on the ground, we walk together toward the house. The boys have run ahead, and are already waiting for us on the porch. As we approach the house, the door opens, and Cora stands there with her own two boys.

"Hello Mercy, it's good to see you," my friend says to me, while her two boys peek out from behind her skirts. They'll get over their shyness right quick when they start running around with my boys, especially when they all start at the school.

"I've missed you," I say as I lean in for a hug. I haven't seen Cora all summer. It's been as busy as ever, but I am grateful we have taken the afternoon to visit our neighbors. Cora takes my basket, and we follow her into her home. Gibby greets Jasper and within seconds the front door bangs behind them as the menfolk go outside.

I follow Cora to her kitchen with Mary Alice in tow behind me. Once there, she places my basket on her counter, and I sit in a chair at the table with Mary Alice at my side.

My basket contains white biscuits and some molasses cookies for dessert. Cora has made chicken and rice for our supper, and I am looking forward to breaking bread with them tonight. I hope my contribution to supper is enjoyed by all. As usual, my food was prepared from the ever-helpful *Aunt Babette's cookbook*. Her book should be a must for all wives, it's such a blessing.

Cora takes my biscuits out of the basket, places them on a plate so she can warm them in the oven later. While she does this, Mary Alice takes Maud Ella from me and places her on the floor where she can watch her as I help Cora. Under Cora's direction, I set the table, and then retrieve a pack of homemade butter from my basket to go with my biscuits.

My stomach growls in anticipation of the chicken and rice Cora is cooking, as it fills her home with its delicious scent. We hear the slam of the front door as all four boys enter the house and tramp into the kitchen, following their noses, which have picked up the aroma of the fragrant supper.

"Is supper ready yet, Ma'am?" Cora's older son Frederick asks, as leader of the little band of ruffians. In the few minutes outside, they have already covered themselves in dust.

"I believe it is!" She says with a smile. "Please fetch your Papas so we can all sit to eat." The front door bangs again as they run to do as they are told. They will return soon enough to fill their bellies.

Cora is lucky to have inherited some lovely flatware that has flower designs pressed into the handles, with plain stoneware plates. She has plenty of kitchenware for us all to eat on. I try to be happy for her, but I wish I had such plates and pretty flatware to share with my guests. Hopefully one day Gibby and I will be able to afford more for our ever-growing family.

The front door slams again as the boys return with their Papas following, and we all crowd around the table, sitting along the trestle benches, which allows for more people to crowd at the table than chairs would.

Cora sets her dinner pot of the chicken with rice, carrots, and broth on the table, and I set my biscuits in a basket down alongside it, with the butter nearby on its own dish. She then places a large serving spoon in the pot, and sits at the long end of the table, across from her husband.

We all clutch each other's hands and wait for the blessing. I am in between Mary Alice, and Earl, with Maud Ella on my lap.

"Lord, we thank you for the food we are about to eat. Please bless us as we eat, play, sleep and spend time together. Thank you for this bounty and the wonderful company we keep" Cora offers the prayer in her Irish brogue, and we all say *Amen* when she is finished. I smile as well, enjoying the moment that a friend is thankful for my family's company. It is good to feel loved and needed.

Everyone releases their neighbor's hands and Cora starts to serve the fathers first then herself and me, and then the children. While she serves, the basket of rolls is passed amongst us, as well as my freshly made butter, and the smell is heavenly. I feed soft bites to Maud Ella, and she chews happily on a piece of bread while she sits on my lap. The kitchen is silent apart from the clinking of flatware on plates, as everyone is famished and would rather eat than talk. There is no small talk for a while until Cora asks me about Wylie School.

"Are the boys excited to attend school this fall?" She asks.

"They for certain are, and they've been practicing on their new slates already," I answer her after I have swallowed a delicious mouthful of tender chicken and gravy. I must ask her for this recipe, or look to see if it is already in my dependable *Aunt Babette's cookbook.*

"I am hoping we can share the burden of getting them to and from school. Both my boys will be going this year, and since we'll be passing your home, perhaps we can take turns taking them to school," she says.

"Most certainly, I look forward to it," I tell her. "I'm always up early, so I can take them to school if you like, and you can pick them up in the afternoon."

"That sounds perfect," Cora smiles. "The boys can walk to your home in the morning, and travel with you from there."

I look over at my boys, who are enjoying their meal, and I am in awe of how fast they are growing. Truth be told, my whole family is growing quickly. Although each day seems to be so long, my time with them is actually quite short. I only spent 17 years with my parents myself, and I still sometimes miss them.

In between bites, Jasper asks Gibby if he has started harvesting.

"Not yet, but I'm planning on it," Gibby replies.

Harvesting takes a long time with our big fields and has to be started early so we don't lose any of the crop. The boys may even help their father a bit this year. Life on a farm means everyone lends a hand as soon as they are able. It may seem young, but other children who don't live on a farm often work in mills, starting as young as eight years old. I shiver, thinking about my boys around all those large, dangerous machines in the mills. I know of one friend that lost a finger when it was in the wrong place. She now has a ring finger with a missing tip due to her mishap. I cannot imagine my boys in such surroundings, and I am grateful they will be at their father's side instead, working on our farm.

Farming might be made up of long hard days, but at least we have our children with us and no mill overseer in charge who cares for profit over the safety of his workforce. The sight of children leaving a mill at the end of the day always makes me sad. The thought of that happening to our children makes me shudder again.

"Mercy do you have a chill?" my friend asks me.

"No, Cora. I'm just thinking of our friend Aurore who lost a finger at the mill, and I thank the Lord our children will not be working there anytime soon," I reply.

"Aye," Jasper says. "The local mills leave a lot to be desired as far as safety goes. I am relieved that a finger is all Aurore lost and that there are not more accidents. Although some mill owners try to treat their employees well, not all of them do." We have maybe a half dozen mills in our town, and more in neighboring towns as well. These mills have sprouted up along the rivers, like brick and clay mushrooms, harnessing the river's energy to create power to run the mills. These mills manufacture and process cloth, and many times you can see what color material they are producing that day by the color of the river downstream. It makes for quite a sight to see a bright red or yellow stream of water flowing by.

The mills have proved quite prosperous, and many of the owners have built homes, even entire villages for the mill workers to live in. It seems generous until one of them can't make the rent. There's not always a lot of sympathy, as there are many other workers ready and willing to take your place in the factory and also in the rented homes. Mill owners also sometimes provide a company store where workers can spend their paycheck or rely on credit to purchase necessities. Many a time a worker will go home with only necessities and nothing clinking in their pocket. Mill workers have to be wary of the convenience of the company store, because they make up for that convenience by charging much higher prices.

One benefit for our family from these mills are that they sell remnants in a store at their factory and these items always sell at a reduced cost, survive theus to clothe our family affordably.

The local mills hire French Canadian immigrants, many of whom do not speak much English. These families tend to stick together, but as our friend Aurore is fluent in French and English, we have become friends. We don't get to see her often as she works so much, and also lives a bit further away in the town of Almyville.

"When you're ready to harvest, let me know and I will do my best to help," Jasper tells my husband.

"And I'll do the same for you, Jasper" Gibby responds. The men often help each other harvest their crops. Hay for their animals, and usually some extra to sell, and corn for cornmeal and other uses. The local schools even give a few weeks off in the fall to allow children to help out on their families' farms. This is truly helpful, and a lot of the time the kids are happy to be away from school.

"I see the Pendletons' house is coming along nicely," Jasper says.

"It certainly is, and Mercy is making a quilt for Alice as well," Gibby tells the O'Dowd's.

Not to be outdone, Cora adds that she is gathering clothes for the children, since they have a boy, Raymond, about the same age as her older son.

Our families finish the meal in companionable silence, and once we're done, the men retreat to the front porch to smoke their pipes, while the children run about on the front lawn. Cora and I wash and dry the dishes then join the men on the front porch.

The O'Dowds have a generous front porch with four porch rockers that invite you to sit for a spell. The four of us rock contentedly together on the porch, enjoying the summer evening.

Smoke from the men's pipes curls around us, and as always I enjoy the fragrance of it. The night is warm, and as the sun sets it envelopes everything in its path with a warm glow. I sigh with pleasure, happy to be with these people and my family.

Earl leaves the other children and runs to Cora. "Mrs. O'Dowd, do you have a jar we could use to hold fireflies, please?"

"But of course, give me a minute and I'll fetch you one!" She smiles at him and leaves the porch to go into the house.

Earl waits with us on the porch while the other children are still running about in the yard. The O'Dowd's family dog runs with the children, barking. The porch door slams as Cora exits the house with a canning jar and lid in her hands.

"Here you go little Earl, but please be sure to let them go once you're finished enjoying them," Cora tells Earl.

"Yes, Ma'am, and thank you," he says as he runs back to the other children like his tail is on fire as they run into the woods.

It's a pleasant night, and we all enjoy listening to the joyful laughter of the children and the peep toads chorusing in the distance. I have Maud Ella on my lap, while I watch Mary Alice chase after her brothers for a glimpse into their jar.

"Maud Ella will be out there chasing fireflies as well before you know it," Cora tells me.

"Time certainly does fly when you're watching children grow," I reply.

We let the children enjoy the warm summer night for a while longer, then call them to the porch.

"Now little Earl, please remember your promise!" Cora reminds my little boy.

Earl holds the canning jar proudly and walks through the children, pausing at each child so they can get a look at the flickering creatures held in the jar. They were quite busy and there are quite a few of the tiny insects swarming in the jar, flickering and searching for a way out. What a shame indeed it would be if they were left in the jar.

Earl comes to my side to show Maud Ella and I the bugs up close. I peer into the jar and see the bright green glow from the little fireflies fluttering. Earl thoughtfully holds it near baby Maud Ella, who reaches a chubby little hand out to smack at the jar. She is only 3 months old and although it is very kind of him to show her, she has no idea what she is looking at.

"Thank you, little Earl, I am sure Maud Ella likes them," I tell my son. He beams his lovely smile at me, with his brown hair in disarray as always, and that cowlick making one side fluff up like a rooster's tail. I watch as he turns the lid a few times, and off it comes, removing the obstacle to the fireflies' freedom.

Earl and I watch as one, then two, then many more fly up and out of the jar and into the warm summer night air. It's just dusk, so we can see them a bit as they look for other fireflies to join.

"I sure am sad to see them go, but I'm happy they are not stuck in the jar," my little boy says to me, very seriously.

"For certain, it's a better life being out there enjoying the wide world, than being stuck in a jar," I agree with him.

Once all the fireflies have escaped, he checks inside the jar again just to be sure. Earl is such a worrier. He flips the jar over, so any that are still left in there will fall out, and none do.

"I think you are all set, Earl. Take the jar to Cora so we can be on our way," I tell my little boy.

Satisfied they are all free, Earl places the jar in Cora's waiting hands.

"Thank you, Ma'am," he says in his little voice.

"What nice manners you have, and you are very welcome," Cora replies.

"Let's go, Earl. Papa is anxious to be on our way home," I tell him, and he spins on his heels and runs to the wagon, waving to his friends as he goes.

We say goodbye to our dear friends and load ourselves into the wagon. Gibby is last to climb up, and once seated flicks the reins to give Smokey the sign to move. I turn to wave to our friends as we start up the hill back to our little homestead.

The O'Dowds wave to us for a while in return from their porch and then retreat into their home. The ride is a short one, and very pleasant on this lovely summer night, and before long we turn into our yard and are home.

Friday, September 14th, 1883

It's harvest time on our little farm. Gibby rose early and was out of the house to meet Jasper at sunrise. It will be a long week for them, but it is good they have each other for company and an extra pair of hands to help. Harvesting takes a long time, with Smokey pulling our wagon along the field, while Gibby and Jasper follow, picking the corn, removing the husk, and throwing it into the wagon. It's tedious work. I will go out around lunchtime and take them something to eat and drink.

On days like these, I make royal ham sandwiches as it is easy for them to eat while they are in the fields.

Once harvested, the corn will be stored in our barn for us to eat, and we will share some with the animals as well, and anything left over will be sold. All these profits add up. Corn, other crops, firewood, my quilts, and any other work Gibby can turn his hands to keep us going.

The Pendletons' house is almost finished, they are waiting on some supplies to complete the task and make it a home worth living in. Gibby has helped quite a bit, and once it is finished I will go over to help Alice get her house in order. It is nice to see everyone has their own task and is willing to help give this family back their home.

Friday, October 19th, 1883

There's a crisp feel to the days now. The frost is coming every morning, and killing off the flowers with its cold bloom each evening.

The twins have been attending the Wylie School for about a month now and they're enjoying it. Mr. Wood is a great teacher, and he makes the children very curious about learning.

The boys spend their evenings sitting at our kitchen table perfecting their letters and writing their names as well. Before long they will be reading the short stories I have read to them since they were born on their own, and may even read the stories out loud to their sisters. I love reading to them and hope they will still allow me to do so, even when they learn to read themselves. It is a fine line for mothers, knowing when to let go. We want our children to grow and be independent of us – but just not yet.

I have been busy this last month, canning what vegetables I can gather from my garden, including potatoes and carrots, and I even have some herbs drying in my kitchen that I will store in glass jars to use over the winter. Anything we can grow and keep is a saving to us. I will trade herbs and canned items with my friends, too. It's good to have a community that shares when they are able to do so.

We were lucky this year to have a large harvest of corn from our fields, as well as some hay. The hay is stored in the upper level of our barn, in storage for Smokey, and perhaps some to sell to anyone who might need some.

Our extra corn will be sold to the local grist mills to be ground for cornmeal. Johnny cakes are made from cornmeal and they're a popular food, as they are great for travelers and easy to cook. Many a traveler will have johnnycakes in his pouch as it is not always easy to find a tavern to dine at, especially in our remote area.

I am excited today as I have gotten word that my parents are visiting tomorrow to see their new granddaughter. It is not often I get to see them, as they live in Exeter, Rhode Island, which is pretty far away.

I grew up there, and met my husband there as well. Gibby's family comes from the same town, and his parents will most likely be anxious to visit soon also. We are lucky to have all four parents living still, something not many families can boast of, and even if we don't get the pleasure of their company often, at least we know they are still with us.

Maud Ella is over six months old, so it will be nice to see my parents and share my children with them. I am of course opening *Aunt Babette's cookbook* to make a delicious meal for them when they arrive tomorrow.

My kitchen is filled with a lovely golden glow from the sun setting through the yellowed leaves of the trees that surround our home. When I look out my kitchen window, I have a lovely view of a little knoll, with a trio of pine trees and Hell Hollow Road in the distance. The view is lovely in the fall with the trees a riot of color.

Saturday, October 20th, 1883

Today my parents are coming for a visit, and I have been toiling hard all morning to get my house in order and prepare a meal. They are arriving midday, and I plan on serving a meal shortly after they get here.

Our home smells wonderful, and chicken, rice and vegetables have been simmering on my cook stove for a while now. I set my table, and then take a minute to confirm everything is in order. Once my table is ready, I check on my children to make sure they are clean and dressed for our visitors.

Earlier in the day Gibby and the boys retrieved fresh water from our spring, and it is now sitting in our ice box chilling. How I wish it were spring, so I could place some lilacs in the center of our table, but there are no lilacs this time of year. In their place I set a few trivets for the bowls of food to rest on, and a few candles for lighting at the ends of the table. It then comes to me, that while my children and home are ready, I am not!

I quickly stride to my bedroom and pull out a dress from my wardrobe to change into. It is my gray dress with the short sleeves, as I am quite warm from cooking and hurrying about to get ready for my folks to arrive. I look into my mirror to straighten my hair, which is pulled back into a bun as usual. I quickly pinch my cheeks to give them some color, then head back to my parlor to join my family as we wait there for our visitors.

In the parlor I find my children stacking blocks for Maud Ella to knock over, and the little room is filled with laughter. I smile as I enter because their happiness is contagious.

Gibby is sitting in his chair and smiles at me as well. He tilts his head, and I look out our front window to see my parents arriving in their hooded carriage. It is a lovely carriage, with a hood that can go up or down according to the weather. Much better than an open wagon like ours. My Mother and Father sit side by side, and as it is a warm day for fall, they have the top down behind them. Mother, who always feels the cold, most likely has a blanket on her lap. They pass by our home, and out of my sight, as they pull into our yard.

"They're here" Bert yells. All the children jump to their feet and head to the back of the house to greet them just as my father pulls on the reins to stop his horse. I stop at the door and ask the children to wait inside, and for Earl to hold Maud Ella.

Gibby goes to my father's horse and leads him to the hitching post we have on the side of our yard. There is also a small water trough near the hitching post, where the horse can drink to refresh himself after his long trek. As Gibby is tethering the horse, my father climbs down and helps my mother down as well. I rush to my parents' side with my arms out wide.

"It is so wonderful to see you, Mama" I cry, feeling like a child again. She pulls me close and clutches me in a warm embrace. We stand like this for a moment while Gibby and my father shake hands in welcome. My father reaches into the carriage and pulls out my mother's travel bag and a box from a local bakery.

"Come inside, the children are anxious to see you both!" I say as my mother, and I pull apart from our embrace.

We walk toward the house, where three little heads are peeking out of a window. My parents see them, and their smiles grow even broader.

"We have been wanting to visit, but it has been so difficult to find the time," my father tells us. My father owns a general store in Exeter, and it's not easy for him to find help to give him a respite from it.

"I understand Papa, I am just happy you both are finally here!" I say as I walk arm in arm with my mother toward the house and our anxious children.

We walk through the door of our home and into our kitchen, where my children are lined up and waiting. Mary Alice is holding Maud Ella, as she often does. Earl always does his best, but Maud Ella's favorite is her older sister.

"Look how much you have all grown!" My mother exclaims, as she kneels and puts her arms out to embrace the children. The twins run into her arms, and I enjoy seeing this display of affection. It's been a while since they last saw their grandparents, and I was worried they may have forgotten them. But my worry was for naught, as they certainly do remember, and they're happy to see them. I smile and wonder if the happiness is also for the small brown paper bags my mother will soon take out of her travel bag.

My mother slowly lets go of the children and stands. Mary Alice then timidly moves closer to her and hands her Maud Ella. Maud Ella is a bit nervous and not as welcoming as her older siblings. She looks at my mother and instantly begins to whimper.

"Well, I see one of your children is not so happy to see me," my mother says with a smile. Understanding that little ones can be a bit hesitant at first with new faces, she hands Maud Ella back to me, which instantly stops her fretting, and turns to give a hug to Mary Alice. After a moment she releases Mary Alice and turns to find the bag my father has brought inside. Once she acquires it, she reaches in to find what the boys are anxiously waiting for. She finds the bags and pulls them out to hand to the children.

I watch as my little boys stand up straight and tall with large smiles on their faces as they wait for their bags of treats. My mother hands each child a bag, and they hug her again in return. The children run into the parlor to open their small brown bags and see what treats they have received. Thankfully my mother knows my worry about hard candy, and there will be only soft chew candy and chocolates in their little bags.

We follow them into the parlor, where Gibby and I sit in our usual chairs, with my parents on the sofa across from us. We pass the afternoon this way, visiting in our parlor and enjoying each other's company.

AS the afternoon comes to an end, my mother and I take our leave and retreat to the kitchen to prepare our meal. We set out glasses for drinks and set dinner upon the table. The last touch is to light the candles. Even though it is not dark, it is a special occasion to have my parents here and I like the ambiance of the lit candles with our meal. I ask my mother to call everyone else in, which she does, and we all sit together to enjoy a meal. The talk is general and then leads into politics as it typically does.

"The President has just passed the Pendleton Act, which allows people to procure jobs based on merit rather than who they might know. It also protects people from losing their employment for political reasons. So far President Arthur is performing well in his new role." My father tells Gibby. They tend to agree on politics more often than not, thankfully, which avoids any unpleasant arguments.

There has been a lot of talk lately about favoritism in government at local levels, even going as high as the White House. I have always felt that the person in charge should try hard to further worthy people, and not just those with the right connections.

President Arthur was promoted to President after President Garfield was shot shortly after being sworn in. He survived the assassination attempt itself, but later succumbed to infections due to the shooting. So did this mean that he truly survived the shooting? I have to think not. Either way, we have a different president than the one originally by the American elected – or should I say the American men? Women still cannot vote, much to the chagrin of many of us ladies. Some strides have been made in the movement for us to be heard, but sadly not enough. I fervently hope my young daughters and future granddaughters will be able to vote when they get older.

While the men are discussing political matters, I think about how I have always enjoyed seeing the fashions of the First Lady, as they trickle down to us eventually. But sadly the President's wife passed two years before he became President, so there is no First Lady at the moment. President Arthur's sister steps into the role when needed, but I think it's very sad there is no one at his side to support him in his duties. I find that in my marriage Gibby and I work as a team. Gibby would have a difficult time farming and raising this family without me, and I would have a hard time farming and raising our family at the same time. We work well together, and I feel bad for those folks who don't have the support of a spouse.

Gibby and my father are discussing how the new act will be more helpful to people in the cities, as we are lucky in the country because politics do not typically interfere with our lives. Many politicians appoint friends and relatives to coveted positions, and this new act will stop that sort of thing. Politicians are a breed apart, and I think we're lucky to live and work far from their reach.

"They are still trying to raise funds for a base for the statue of liberty," My mother tells us, stopping the tedious talk of politics by changing the subject swiftly.

"I find it hard to donate to anyone other than the church when I struggle to feed my own family. Why should I help them build a base for a statue I'll probably never see?" Gibby replies. My father nods his head in agreement, not talking because he is enjoying his dinner too much. I smile at this, as it makes me happy to cook for my family.

The country of France gave us a statue loaded with symbolism. It's a very tall statue of a woman in robes, with one foot forward and a broken shackle at her ankle. This broken shackle symbolizes the abolition of slavery in our country, which in my mind is a wonderful thing. The lady is holding a book with the roman numerals for July 4th, 1776, which of course is the day of our independence from England, and she holds a torch as if to light the way to our shores. The symbolism probably says as much about the way the French feel about the British as it does about the abolition of slavery, but either way she is to be called the Statue of Liberty. This statue is to be a joint venture between France and the people of America, with our country's contribution being the construction of a base big and sturdy enough for her to stand on.

It has been quite difficult to raise funds in our country, as we are still recovering from war and there's not a lot of money left over for our people to support something that does not feed or help our own families. I am hoping some of America's wealthier citizens will step up a bit more to finance this statue, as I think she will be a formidable sight for ships sailing into New York Harbor. It's a sight I would like to see for myself one day. Her position in the harbor will be a welcoming sight for immigrants sailing past her when arriving in our country via Ellis Island, which is only a mile or so away from the statue.

Her arm holding the torch has been on display in Madison Park, New York for quite a while now, with the hopes people will donate to the cause when they see the sculpture in person. I am sure it is a sight to behold, and hopefully it will make people reach into their own pockets to donate.

Dinner is over before long, and we move on to dessert, which is a cake that my mother has brought from a bakery in my hometown, which I have always enjoyed. As well as being a delicious treat, I am also happy that I was relieved of creating a dessert for us all.

The visit is a lovely one, and before we know it, we are embracing each other, and my parents are climbing back into their little carriage for the ride home. It is always wonderful to see them, and my little family waves to them until they are out of sight, and then we slowly walk back into our home together.

Monday, October 22nd, 1883

Today is the day the Pendleton family finally moves into their new home. After church services yesterday, Gibby spent the day helping Alfred Pendleton with last-minute details. All in all, the house was rebuilt quite quickly, and we are planning on visiting this afternoon to see if they need any assistance. I also want to give them the quilt I have sewed for them.

We eat our dinner early, then get into our wagon to travel to their home, which is only a short distance away. As we arrive, we join a few other town folks who are already there. The house is a den of activity, with people inside and out in the yard. The boys jump down to join other children playing, while we walk to the front porch, with the girls following. I carry my quilt.

"Hello, Gibby and Mercy!" Alice says with a smile. She is an older woman with a large bosom and gray hair, who also makes lovely quilts herself. I only hope my quilt is to her standards.

"Hello Alice, I brought you a quilt to keep you warm on the winter nights. I hope you like it," I tell her as I hand the large, colorful quilt to her, and she looks at it closely.

"On Mercy, it looks wonderful! And such pretty fabric. I haven't had a moment in the day to make one for myself, so this is a most welcome gift. And one that will keep us warm this winter.

Thank you!" She tells me, her gratitude showing in her face. I beam within, happy that I went forward with making it even though I worried it would not be good enough to give to such a seamstress as Alice.

"Please come in and see our new home." She says, standing aside to let us pass. The front room is aglow with lanterns, and pretty much already in order. The Pendletons must have been quite busy today! We walk on through to the new kitchen, also ablaze with lanterns and smelling like fresh-cut wood. Alice offers us a glass of lemonade, as she has a tray with glasses on her table for her house guests.

Gibby and I take the glasses she hands to us, and we both take a sip of the cool refreshing drink.

"I am so indebted to our townsfolk for getting us back into our home, and so quickly," Alice tells us.

"I fear we can never repay this debt, but we will be sure to help others whenever they need it," her husband Peter chimes in.

"We are just happy to help, and even more happy that it was only a home that was ruined in the fire," Gibby tells them, which elicits murmurs of agreement throughout the kitchen.

We stay a while longer, with Gibby visiting the men, while I follow Alice to their bedroom to help her unpack.

Once she is settled in, we say our goodbyes and leave them for their first night in their newly rebuilt home. I am sure all the townsfolk that helped will enjoy a contented night's sleep after playing their part in returning the family to their home.

Thursday, November 29th, 1883

The leaves have fallen, and the cold is settling in. It is a fear of mine that the cool air will bring on another round of diphtheria.

Oh, how a mother worries!

I haven't forgotten all the other grief-stricken mothers with whom I have stood by the side of a small grave, and I fervently hope it will never be me. Every spring that blooms with all my children still by my side makes me relieved.

Winters are often long, cold and snowy, and with the added fear of illness it's no wonder I look forward to spring and enjoy it so much when it comes! I am certain I am not alone in my little town with these feelings, as most mothers I know have the same worries.

We spent Thanksgiving with our neighbors Cora and Jasper, and the holiday passed quickly. It was enjoyable to enjoy the companionship of our friends in our cozy little home.

We woke this morning to a light snow, and I knew the boys would be anxious to be outside and play. There looked to be enough snow to slide down the hill behind our home and more than enough snow for a good snowball fight. They can be at these antics for hours, and I will end up watching from the warmth of our home, through the windows as they coat each other with snow.

Monday, January 14th, 1884

We've had a glorious Christmas. I was very pleased with my gift-giving this year, as I was able to find the time to embroider a few samplers for my dear friends Cora and Delphine.

The boys got some books to sharpen their reading skills, as well as some metal soldiers and a cannon. I will never understand the fascination with guns or cannons, but it is always a well-received gift for little boys. If you don't give them a toy gun to play with, they will simply make one with their fingers or a stick they find on the ground in the forest. I have simply given up on trying to protect them from violence.

I was born at the start of the civil war, in 1861, and although I do not remember the horrors of war, I have been educated fully by my parents. It's politicians at work again. They create wars, but it is the ordinary folks who suffer.

One of the major battles of the Civil War was in Gettysburg, Pennsylvania, during the summer. When I was older my father told me stories of the battle, and how many died from infected wounds if they didn't die immediately. Many soldiers perished in the fields, along with the horses that they rode into battle. It was horrifying to hear about the sights and the smell of the dead that drifted for miles on the wind after the battle.

My father often told me it was the worst of all wars because it was fought against our own citizens. There were brothers on opposing sides, fighting one another. I always listened attentively when he spoke of such matters.

I cannot imagine the anguish of a mother knowing her son is off fighting in a war, and hope that I never have to. I only hope our country has learned from this grisly and devastating war and that such a thing will never be repeated. One can only hope. So it was only natural that I should try to shield my children from guns, but sadly it didn't work, as they just pick up a stick that looks like a gun and shout "bang!" at one another.

There was another snowstorm during the night, adding to the snow that was already on the ground, and we now have about eight inches of it in our yard. There's a small hill above our house that the children love to slide down. We have two runner sleds which I inherited from my parents when they got past the age of wanting to spend much time in the snow. They are wooden sleds with metal rails, with a long rope to pull them back up the hill.

A long day of sledding and snowball throwing always tuckers the boys out for a long night's sleep. I always find it amazing how much a day spent in the fresh air makes children sleep so well—even infants!

The boys went out a little while ago with Gibby to play, and now we've all joined the twins outside to spend a while frolicking in the crisp, white snow. I love to see the boys enjoying themselves, with big grins on their faces as they run up the hill and slide down it over and over. I am enjoying watching the boys when Earl runs to my side.

"Mama, if I am careful may I please take Mary Alice for a ride down the hill?" he asks.

"If you are careful and if she wants to go, then sure you can," I reply, smiling back at him. "That is very thoughtful of you, Earl."

"Thank you, Mama," Earl says as he reaches his hand out to take Mary Alice's. She puts her hand in his and walks up the small hill with him. Earl is pulling the sled with his other hand, and when they reach the top, he turns it, so the sled is facing down the hill. He then helps Mary Alice onto the sled and sits behind her. Bert, who's been watching all this, goes to Earl's side and gives him a gentle push so he can slide down the hill carefully instead of taking his usual headlong rush. I watch this scene between siblings unfold and I smile. I am happy my boys are turning out to be so thoughtful and kind.

Once they reach the bottom, Earl jumps off the sled, grabs the rope, and takes Mary Alice, who is still seated on the sled, back to the top of the hill so they can do it all over again. They repeat this many more times as the sun starts to fade.

When it's getting too dark to see properly, I tell them to come inside and warm themselves and Mary Alice in front of the fire.

Friday, February 8th, 1884

I awake to total silence. The kind of total, muffled silence you only get when the world is covered in snow. From the warm vantage of my bed, I look out my window and can see the trees are once again covered with snow. Their branches are drooping from the weight of it. Another snowstorm! I am alone in my bed. Gibby must be already up and stoking our fire to keep the house warm. I take a second to enjoy the warmth from Grandma Antonia's blanket, then get out of my warm bed and quickly use my chamber pot. I don't want to trudge to the outhouse without a path being cut through the snow, and as always am grateful for my little chamber pot. I carefully put the chamber pot back under my bed, to be emptied as soon as there's a path outside. It is a bit chilly in my room, and I quickly pull on a warm woolen dress and some thick wool socks.

It has been an easy winter so far, with sunny days and snow, and the children will be very excited this morning to see this wonderland.

I head to the kitchen, where Gibby already has a nice fire glowing. The kitchen is warm and welcoming.

"Good morning Mercy."

"Good morning," I reply

"It snowed about seven inches last night, and I've already shoveled a path to the outhouse," he tells me.

"Thank you, Gibby. The children will be excited to see more snow" I answer.

"They will until they're old enough to shovel paths with me," he smiles, happy that by next winter they'll be helping and no doubt grateful that it's almost spring and hopefully we won't be getting much more snow.

"That's true, but let's take them sledding again after chores are done."

"Sounds like a great idea" He agrees.

I start our usual breakfast of eggs and buttered bread, while Gibby wakes the children so they can join us. Once we have all eaten, everyone returns to their rooms to dress in layers to go outside to complete their chores. There are paths to be shoveled, animals to be fed and chamber pots to be emptied.

It is afternoon and we are finally all done cleaning from the snowstorm when we hear the muffled sound of horses' hooves in the snow. Delphine and Everett, with their girls, arrive in their put-together sleigh… which is made up from boxes on metal runners pulled by their team of horses. These homemade sleighs are a delight, and I am very excited to see our friends appear with theirs. Any tiredness I am feeling disappears with at the sight of the horses, their manes flying in the wind, hooves kicking up snow, as they come trotting into my yard, trailed by the box sleigh.

"Hello, Culver Family!" I exclaim in delight!

"Hello, Mercy, Hello Gibby," Delphine replies with her big smile.

My children, who are not the slightest bit tired from the morning's chores, jump onto the back of the sleigh, joining the Culver daughters, and then help Mary Alice up as well. I place Maud Ella in Mary Alice's arms and step back from the sleigh.

"I'll be back in one minute," I tell the merry group as I hasten back to the house to grab some fresh mittens and blankets. These sleigh rides can get a bit cold, sitting in one place with the wind blowing in your face. A blanket to bundle up in is welcome indeed. I know for certain that Delphine has blankets as well, but when it is cold you can never have too many layers of warmth to cover yourself with. I walk out through the back door and head back to the waiting sleigh.

Gibby is waiting by the side of the sleigh for me and helps me in, where I join Delphine and the children.

"Where would you like to take a ride?" asks Everett.

Seeing as we have a free afternoon, I ask to do a loop through town. Everett swings the sleigh around and the horses whisk us out of our hollow and onto Ekonk Hill. The horses trot along, and the blankets that Delphine and I have thought to bring keep all of us cozy. Delphine and I sit with the children, while Gibby and Everett are on the bench seat above us. The landscape surrounding us is breathtaking, and everything—including the sky, which looks to be promising more snow—is the same light gray. Trees, roads, and homesteads are covered in snow, muffling all sound and wrapping us in a silent winter fairyland. Tree branches laden with snow make a canopy over the road, bringing the forest even closer to us. Over the snow-covered roads we glide, thankful that others have traveled through before us, or we wouldn't even know for sure where the road was! We follow their tracks into town, where many are still shoveling and clearing the snow.

The village of Oneco looks neat and clean under its fresh blanket of snow, and a dark gray ribbon of smoke curls into the gray sky from almost every chimney. Folks are hard at work trying to keep their homes warm, making me think that we might also make some coin from people needing firewood. I am always thinking of ways to earn extra coin for our household, as a farmer can never grow enough to maintain a family these days. Those thoughts whisk out of my head as Everett drives us past his house and takes a few turns until we are onto Newport Road past Whitford's, which is quite busy, then past many more homes, all emitting that same ribbon of smoke from a hard-working chimney. We pass Kenyon's store and tavern where a few other homemade sleighs sit in the yard, then continue on. It is a lovely smooth ride, and we are all nice and warm clutched together wrapped in our blankets. The boys are sitting on the end by themselves, as they are not cold yet, they're just excited to be out and about in a sleigh.

Soon we turn onto Porter Pond and then onto Cedar Swamp Road, which will take us back to our home. We glide past many homesteads, as surprisingly this area is settled quite a bit. The ride has taken a few hours and the little ones have been lulled to sleep by the gentle movement of the sleigh. We arrive home as the sun begins to set, casting a lovely rose pink glow across the otherwise monochrome landscape. Everett turns the team into our yard, and once the sleigh comes to a stop, the children jump out into the snow. The men step from the front of the box sleigh, help the little girls out first, and then Delphine and I, until the sleigh is empty.

Delphine takes her girls to use our privy, as they still have a return ride to their home. I ask her if she would like to stay for a visit, but Everett tells me he still needs to get the horses home and cooled down, fed then turned into their stalls.

We hug each other, and when it is my turn to hug Delphine, I kiss my dear friend on her cheek as well. The Culvers climb back into their sleigh, with Delphine returning to her place at the side of her husband, and the girls in the back wrapping themselves in the blankets. All at once they are off up the road towards their home, waving to us until they are out of sight.

Thursday, May 8th, 1884

Winter is officially behind us at last, and it was an easier one than most. There was not a lot of illness in our home this winter either, which is a wonderful blessing.

Today is Maud Ella's first birthday. She is a delightful child, and so mild-mannered. I have been making a small cake for her, using a recipe from my faithful *Aunt Babette's cookbook.* My parents and Gibby's have sent gifts for Maud Ella through the mail, and she has a new book and a new dress that my mother has made for her. I plan on serving a roast ham with potatoes and carrots, with the cake as dessert. I enjoy baking much more than cooking, as I tend to have a sweet tooth, and enjoy my home made confectionaries! I have enjoyed preparing for Maud Ella's birthday.

The day has been a warm one, and my lilacs are in bloom. I will cut some sprigs as always to place on our table, and make it festive and filled with color. The fragrance of the lilacs is always a welcome addition as well.

Gibby is out, as always, chopping firewood. It's a never-ending task, and a good filler of his time until planting season starts. I'm sure Gibby is looking forward to a time when the twins can join him in the field, for their company as well as their help.

Today the boys are at school, so it is just us girls at home this afternoon. Mary Alice has been playing with her sister so I can attend to the cooking and baking.

I have also been feeling a little tired, and I've started to wonder if I am with child again. Time will surely tell.

Friday, July 4th, 1884

I am truly with child again, and I'm expected to deliver sometime next February. It has been an easy pregnancy so far, thankfully. My boys are now five years old and they're a delight to all who meet them. I am so proud of their manners, as well as their intelligence and kindness. They will surely be wonderful men someday! I surely hope so, anyways. The girls are bright and precocious as well. Mary Alice is quite anxious to go with her brothers to school. She'll be joining them soon enough, but Maud Ella has some time to go yet. I am proud that my children will go to school and will not be working in a factory like some of the less fortunate children.

Last winter there was a small outbreak of diphtheria, which we were very lucky to avoid, along with our other friends. The feeling of gratefulness that my loved ones are happy and healthy is overwhelming. I cannot even think about the sadness other mothers in our town have lived through. But enough morbid thoughts. It is best not to worry about something you cannot control or change.

We have been lucky to have two consecutive good harvests. Between the harvests, my quilts, and the firewood, we are surviving. Gibby was a sea captain before I met him, and had a bit of savings from that livelihood, which got us our homestead. He spent many years traveling up and down the coast delivering cotton to the mills in our area from the south. He was a good saver, and with that savings, we are fortunate to own our own land and our home. Many others rent or live in Company housing. To own acreage and home is lucky indeed.

We are getting ready to leave for a picnic in town by the pond for the July Fourth holiday. This is an exciting holiday, with a grand picnic in the field by the river that widens out at that point until it looks more like a pond, ending with a small firework display over the water. The children love the fireworks, as it is the only time of year they see the large colorful flowers of fire in the sky and reflected in the water. It is truly one of the most exciting days of the year, and all the children have been waiting for it. It is also one of the rare times we travel at night as a family. I have as usual depended upon Aunt Babette for our picnic feast. I will be preparing my royal ham sandwiches, as they travel well, along with lots of other picnic food, and packing blankets for us to sit on as well. We will travel with the O'Dowds and meet the Culvers at the field.

The O'Dowds walk the short distance to our home to travel with us to the festivities. Once they arrive, we load up and set off on our way, Gibby and Jasper in front and Cora and I sitting in the back with the children. The day is lovely and sunny with a beautiful sky overhead filled with large white gossamer clouds suspended over us, moving on a light wind. Flowers are in bloom at almost all the homes we pass. Some homesteads have large trees in their yards that are very round in shape since they are mostly alone on the property and have room to spread out, as all other trees have been cut for firewood or wood to make the home. Many homes have the American flag hanging from the porch, or from an open window, the flags hardly stirring in the warm afternoon.

I am wearing one of my lighter dresses, short sleeved with a high collar. My hair is drawn up in my usual bun to keep it off my neck. The only movement in the warm air is the modest breeze created by our movement in the wagon that moves along the road at a steady pace.

We travel into the village of Oneco, where we turn into the large field along the river.

This river is where most of the ice is harvested for many ice boxes in the winter, but in summer it is a delightful respite from warm weather. The river is a dependable benefactor for all seasons, providing ice in the winter, swimming in the summer as well as a regular supply of fish. Gibby directs Smokey to an open area to park, and once the wagon comes to a halt we disembark to find a space to spend the afternoon.

We set up on a blanket, where the adults are happy to just sit a while as the children run off to play. We wait a short time for the Culvers to join us, and finally they arrive. Now we're all here, six adults, while the children wait to go for a swim. We all walk to the river's edge and the boys run in full steam, without a second to check the water temperature. The girls tiptoe in more cautiously, but within a few minutes all the children are in the water, with their parents watching them closely. From a few years of this tradition, my boys have learned how to swim a bit, and they get better each year. We are lucky to have a lovely pond below our homestead as well, where the boys also get to practice their strokes. After an hour of frolicking in the water, we take the children back to our blanket so we can eat our dinner. Each family has brought their own food, but we pass about cookies to share for dessert. The children love trying each variety, and we settle back on our blankets to wait for the firework show to begin.

Before long the sky is illuminated with bursts of color high above, the light from the fireworks coloring us, making us glow. I look over and see all of my children, heads tilted back gazing into the sky, their faces changing in hue to match whatever color firework is blooming. I smile contentedly and turn my gaze into the sky to enjoy the show.

The display is soon over, and our three families pack our blankets and leftover picnic food and place it in our respective wagons. The men round up the exhausted children, and we say our goodbyes to the Culvers as we head home with the O'Dowds and wait in the line to leave the field with the rest of the town folks. It's now nighttime, so we'll drive the O'Dowds directly to their homestead, so they do not have to walk there from ours in the dark.

We travel in the glow of a sickle moon and the light from our wagon's lanterns, guiding us home.

Thursday, August 7th, 1884

It is a warm summer's day, and the children and I are sitting in the shade in front of our home when I look outside my window to see a negro man walk into our yard. He is dressed in dirty clothes that have been repaired with patches of other material in places, with still more holes in other areas. Wearing a hat to block the sun, he carries a stick with a large bag hanging from it, as he looks toward our house. Just as I'm about to go outside to ask what he's doing in our yard, I see Gibby approaching him. They talk for a while, and then the man heads to our barn. I watch as Gibby walks to our back door, and I meet him in the kitchen.

"Another former slave, Gibby?" I ask him.

"Aye. He is asking if he can stay in our barn and help with harvesting to earn some coin." Gibby could use the help, as it looks to be a great harvest year, and as Jasper always says, "many hands make light work".

"Well that was fortuitous timing," I tell him.

"Most definitely is. He stopped at Whitford's first, and Mr. Whitford told him we might be needing a hand," Gibby says. "He'll stay in the barn at night, and help harvest during the day. I told him I can't afford to pay much, but we can feed and shelter him, which is fine by him. But be careful while he's here. We never know who these travelers truly are. I reckon he'll be happy to have some food and a roof over his head even if he doesn't earn much for working with us. We also must take care, as not everyone is as kind to colored people."

My husband is referring to the fact that there are some people in town who are downright mean to coloreds, and we have to be careful they don't treat us the same for taking one in. It sure is a shame that we have to tread carefully about being kind to another person, but sadly that's the way it is.

We've had a few of these former slaves help at harvest over the years, and we haven't had any trouble with the slaves or our townsfolk yet, but it is best to be prudent. Jasper has had a favorable year as well, so the traveler will help at both farms. It is a favorable arrangement for all.

The man does indeed turn out to be from the south, sadly with no family. He's traveling through the northern states hoping to find a permanent place to stay. He is grateful for a place to lay his head at night and food to fill his belly. He seems friendly enough, and I enjoy hearing about his exploits. Before you know it, he's sitting at our table for supper most evenings, enthralling the children with his stories.

I am happy the children are observing someone a bit different from them, as I want them to grow to be good people, and not dislike someone because they are a different color. The civil war ended many years ago, but it's still a difficult life for a colored person. I have never had an issue with color myself, and I find this man kindly and well-disposed, and am glad we can help him a bit.

Wednesday, September 3rd, 1884

The summer has come to an end, and what a lovely summer it was. A season full of picnics, visits with friends and typical everyday chores. It was a perfect summer weather-wise, and we are going to have a sizable crop this year, praise God. The trees have just started to change to rust and bright yellow, making the landscape glow with color. Reds, oranges, yellows and even some of those pink leaves I always see at this time of the year surround us as the trees look like exaggerated flowers through our neighbor's yard and all over the town.

The negro man, whose name we discovered is Frank, has been invaluable. He helps Gibby and Jasper every day, and Jasper has gotten quite friendly with him. I think the men have something in common, as the townsfolk are not always accepting and kind to the O'Dowds as immigrants, and Jasper knows it's much worse for a colored man.

Frank travels between our homes, staying in our barns and dining at our tables, which is not the sort of thing that's always accepted by other townsfolk. Gibby is not chastised much as he is older and respected for having been a sea captain for many years. I wish I could say the same for the O'Dowds. Jasper has to take care if going to a tavern, as once liquor is added to the mix, things can turn violent.

The O'Dowds have even had a note tacked to their door warning them not to be so kind to coloreds, but they simply took the paper down and carried on. Gibby's status means that we have not received the same kind of warning, thankfully. I am right proud of both families for being kind to Frank, and hopefully we will change other people's views one day.

In the meantime, we continue to show kindness to this man, who has little more than the clothes he stands up in. He has not seen much happiness in his life, and the way he's been treated saddens me. I hope that the way we treat Frank guides our children, so that they can perhaps change this wrong for future generations.

While breaking bread with us, Frank tells us of his life on a plantation down south. I watch as the children listen wide-eyed about how he lived in a tiny shack with other slaves, and how he worked in the fields and in the stables too. He tells tales of other slave children as well as the horses he took care of. Thankfully his stories are tame. I am sure he has more horrifying tales, and I am happy he spares us them. It pains me to know how much people like Frank have suffered.

Harvesting season is soon over, and Jasper and Gibby are able to give him coin, and he happily heads off on his travels once again. I am grateful and proud that our two families showed him kindness, and I hope wherever he lands he finally finds happiness.

We are only in this world once, we must do our best to find joy where and when we can, no matter our skin color or station in life.

Saturday, November 1st, 1884

The twins have been attending school for almost two months, and they love it. They are hungry for stories, and they learn their letters and do their sums.

Cora and I take turns getting all the boys to and from school. Gibby or I take them to the little school on Ekonk Hill, then the O'Dowds pick them up at the end of the day.

Mr. Wood is wonderful, and thankfully he's a patient man with my rambunctious boys. Not all school teachers are so kind, there are stories of raw knuckles from being rapped with a ruler, and sore ears from being pulled frequently. I am grateful my twins are not subjected to this treatment, and instead jump out of bed each day, eager to attend school with a new appetite for learning.

My pregnancy is progressing well, and it is a blessing I feel so well, but I am lucky it's not harvest time and Gibby can assist me when I need it. But so far I am feeling fine, and I'm looking forward to adding to my family once again.

Marnie Reynolds-Bourque

Wednesday, November 5th, 1884

We voted in a new President yesterday—or should I say the menfolk did. Gibby and I took a ride into town with the children today to see who had won.

Women can still not vote, so Gibby was the only one to put a vote in the ballot box yesterday.

Our new President is Grover Cleveland, who despite a scandal and improper behavior attaching to his name will now be running our country. They say this newly elected President forced himself on a woman years ago and got her with a child. He later had the child removed from her and had her committed to an asylum. She was denigrated as a loose woman after that and has had the most difficult of lives. I think perhaps he was lucky that women couldn't vote in this election as he for certain would not have gotten my vote. Let's hope he runs the country better than he does his personal life.

As for voting, this remains a sore spot with me, as I read about politics in our daily paper and would like to have the right to cast my vote.

There are wonderful women fighting for our right to vote, and I am thankful to them. In 1872 one brave woman actually went to the polls and voted in the election. So brave of her! Her name was Susan

B. Anthony, and she marched right into where men were voting along with 14 other women and voted too! Sadly they were arrested for their actions, but I am hoping this will bring more attention to our plight. We haven't made a lot of progress, as the main organization for women's suffrage has split into two because they cannot agree. To me, that seems foolhardy, as there is always strength in numbers. But the group went their separate ways over disagreements about race and letting black folks vote as well. We will see if this split hurts the movement in any way, but I believe it will, which is a shame.

I watch the progress of American society from my sleepy little town and hope for a better future for my daughters and granddaughters. It would be nice to have our voices heard one day in the same manner as the menfolk. There are still demonstrations and marches, but it hasn't really made much of a difference as yet.

Saturday, December 20th, 1884

It'll be Christmas in a week and today we're going out to find our Christmas tree. There's a little pine grove on the knoll above our home, and I think we're bound to find something suitable up there.

I am in the kitchen trying to get my excited children bundled up for our adventure when Gibby comes to the back door brandishing a saw.

"I'm ready to go. Are you all set?" He asks, standing at the door so he doesn't bring any snow into our home.

"We most certainly are!" I respond as I place a hat upon Mary Alice's head, then one for Maud Ella. The twins, who have gotten ready themselves, yell and run out to join Gibby, and we follow their trail.

It is a bright winter's day outside. There was a light snowfall last night, adding to what was already on the ground, so we have decided to take both sleighs with runners so any children can ride on one if they get tired, or even if they just want to! The other sleigh will carry the tree back to our home. It'll be so much easier to put the tree on the sled and pull it along, rather than dragging it, covering it with snow and breaking branches as we drag it home by hand.

There's an older layer of snow under last night's light dusting that crunches noisily as we walk, and sometimes the icy crust gives way and we fall knee-deep into the powdery snow beneath it. I am glad I have my tall boots on under my skirts, otherwise I'd be pretty cold already. The boys have no such worries as they zig-zag along making snow balls and throwing them at one another. I pull an empty sled behind me, while Gibby pulls a sled with the girls riding on it.

It is a crisp day, and I am enjoying being outside. Sometimes the sun peeks through the clouds and warms us a little. We reach the grove in no time at all and take a look to see what there is. We have to keep in mind what will fit in the parlor of our little home. One year we got a tree that was too large, and it was difficult to move around in our parlor, and Gibby had to cut the top off to make it fit!

"Can you boys see anything?" Gibby calls out to the twins, as they have naturally reached the grove first and are already scouting out prospects. There are quite a few pine trees, all at different heights, and the boys disappear out of sight, then reappear as they run between the pines excitedly.

"Mama, Papa! Over here!" Bert yells. We make our way over to a nicely shaped little tree. It's taller than Bert but not too tall to fit in our room. Gibby inspects the tree.

"It's got a nice shape, Bert, and no large gaps between the branches. But are you sure you want to pick one out this quickly? Let's look around a bit more. What do you say, Earl?" Gibby turns to the other twin.

Bert looks at Earl, and Earl looks a bit overwhelmed. The more sensitive of my two boys, he is a pleaser. He wouldn't want to go against Bert, and as Bert has already chosen a tree, he will agree with his twin.

"I think Earl might like the tree as well," I say, "and honestly there's a whole lot of them that look pretty much the same," It's true. The young saplings are almost the same height and shape, as they have not grown tall enough to crowd each other in and hinder growth. They are twins of a sort, only Christmas trees. Earl smiles at my statement, and I return his smile, knowing he is happy to be relieved of making a fuss.

Gibby takes a few turns around the field to make sure there's nothing better, returns to us and smiles.

"I do believe we have found our tree!" he proclaims, and at this the boys jump around us with large smiles across their faces, enjoying the success of finding the right tree.

Gibby bends down to saw through the little trunk, and once he's so he grabs it by the base, places it on one of the sleds starts to pull it back the way we came. I take over with the other sled, pulling the girls home who are still on the sled.

"Hold onto the edges girls, and I'll give you a ride," I tell my daughters, who smile at me. At this Earl who was helping to guide the Christmas tree on the sled with Bert, releases it and runs over to us.

"Can I pull them, Mama?" he asks me. "And then when we reach the hill, we can all slide down!"

"Why thank you, Earl, yes you may," I answer him, placing the rope into his little hand, to pull the sled. "Just take care of your sisters."

"I will, Mama," he assures me, and he takes the rope to pull them along. It is a charming sight, looking at my children, and a lovely memory we are making. The six of us enjoying a warm winter day in a pretty forest, gathering our tree for the holiday. As always I stand back for a moment to take it in, then follow the trail the little sled carrying my daughters is making. It is not a long walk back to our home, and before we know it we are at the top of the little hill leading down the slope to our yard. Earl pushes his sisters toward the front of the sled to make room for himself. He takes the rope and pulls it over the girls' heads, then sits behind them, still holding the rope in his hands.

"I'll give you a push!" yells Bert, dropping his part of the tree and running over to his brother.

"Not too hard a push," I remind him, knowing how exuberant he can be. He reaches his waiting siblings and gives them a nice strong push sending them smoothly down the hill, and we watch their progress until they come to a standstill in the yard behind our home.

"Nicely done Bert," I tell him, and he gives me a large smile before running after the others.

Gibby and I follow their trail down into our yard. Gibby does his best to shake any remaining snow from the tree and then brings it into our home to set up. We have a wooden tree stand which Gibby made, in which he will stand the tree in. It works fairly well as long as we don't get a tree that's too large and makes it top-heavy.

While he takes care of this task, I watch my children play in the snow. Now that the other sleigh no longer has the tree on it, the twins are racing each other down the hill as I hold Maud Ella. As they run back up the hill to do it again, I think of how well they will sleep tonight. Mary Alice takes a few turns with them as well but soon comes to my side, tired from the activity and feeling the cold. It is hard work running back up the hill in the snow, and it has been a long day for her.

"A few more turns, then please put the sleds back in the barn and come inside," I tell the boys.

"Yes Mama," they respond happily.

Mary Alice and I walk to our back door in the snow, happy to return to the warmth of our home and decorate our tree.

I walk inside with the girls, and we take off our outer clothes and head to the parlor to see how Gibby is faring. We find him under the tree, and I then hear a few curse words.

"Do you need some help?" I ask my husband.

"I most certainly do! Please hold the tree so I can tighten it. It's much easier with two people." He tells me, his voice muffled. Walking to the tree quickly, I look to see where I can hold the trunk to help. I see a spot through the branches and take a hold of it, then stand patiently while he tightens the stand to hold the tree upright. He finishes quickly as it is much easier for him to work when the tree is not shifting. He stands as I let go of the tree.

Now that I don't have to hold it, I go to the trunk in our room which holds the few ornaments we have. Many of them were made by my children from pine cones, but there are a few other homemade ones from earlier days as well. It is a small collection, to say the least. Lastly, there is a garland I made from a pretty ribbon to go round the tree. I gather the box containing all our holiday items and return to the parlor, where I set the box down, then I go to the rear door to call the boys in. I know they will not want to miss trimming the tree. Within a few minutes, they arrive, making a ruckus as they always do, taking their outer clothes off and then placing them on the pegs that we have on the wall at their height.

While they are doing this, I walk to my kitchen and grab the plate of cinnamon cookies I made for everyone to enjoy while we decorate. I return to find Gibby stoking a lovely fire, creating a wonderful warmth in our parlor. The boys are close to him, warming themselves from the cold outside. We ate a late lunch, so the cookies are a treat and will hold them over until morning.

I head to the tree and call the children who join me, and we look into the box for ornaments to hang. I hand Mary Alice a few ornaments, and she places them on the lower branches. We enjoy working together, and there is a lot of giggling and happy smiles.

Once we're done, Gibby and I sit in our chairs, while the children play at our feet like they always do. The fire blazes, the lamps glow and we relax for the night.

Tuesday, January 20th, 1885

We all enjoyed the holidays, with the children receiving new books to read as well as a few toys. We spent Christmas holed up in our warm house as the snow fell heavily outside our window. It's another cold day, and I'm inside sewing some shirts for my boys. They're growing so fast I can hardly keep up.

We've heard that one of the grist mills we have in town is closing. It's sad news, because a grist mill is where we local residents get grain which is ground down to make our bread.

Typically, the mill owners grind their grain and sell it in the local stores, or to the taverns for bread. I've been to a few grist mills, and they are picturesque as well as efficient. The large water wheel drops waterfalls to spin the large wheel, which in turn generates the power to turn the wheel grinding the grain, which is quite loud. When we visit to purchase grain, the children will place their hands over their ears to drown out the noise, and I sometimes have to yell at the owner in our conversations to make myself heard.

I always feel a bit sad when a business closes, and people are put out of work. Sometimes they close because their methods are outdated, as inventors create something more efficient to take its place. Either way, it is a sad day when a water wheel comes to a halt.

Saturday, February 28th, 1885

On the fifteenth of this month I birthed another babe, with the usual help from Cora and Delphine. Luckily, my deliveries seem to go easier than many other ladies in town.

This babe is a boy and has been named Charles Adam, and we are now a family of seven.

My happiness with my new son is soon overshadowed by the news that the dreaded diphtheria has returned to our town. Our boys go to school with others now, and Earl has started feeling unwell. I am beside myself with worry that my healthy, happy little boy is feeling ill, and we have moved the other children into our bed, in order to keep him away from the others, but I fear the damage may already have been done.

Sunday, March 8th, 1885

The damage has indeed been done, and it has been a terribly long week in our home.

Gibby and I are in my children's bedroom, sitting at the side of their bed. I am holding Earl's little hand in mine. Sometimes it's sweaty, sometimes it's clammy as the fever comes and goes. My boy is a fighter, and Gibby keeps on dunking a cloth into the cold water pitcher and wringing it out to place gently onto little Earl's forehead.

It looks as though Earl has caught the dreaded diphtheria, as many of his classmates have had it. Most have recovered, thankfully, and I am trying to be hopeful he will as well. He coughs relentlessly, his little body shaking with the violence of the coughs. Delirious with fever, he talks nonsense.

I look beyond my son, and past Gibby to the window showing that it's a bright sunny day outside. How can it be sunny when we are suffering so much inside this dreary room?

Gibby and I are beside ourselves, taking turns at night to stay by his side as his nursemaids. I am either nursing little Charles or tending to Earl, whose fever has taken a turn for the worse and we can't seem to break it.

Oh merciful heavens, please help my boy!

If it's not enough that one of my beloved boys is sick, Bert has started with the coughing too. The girls are both now in our room on a cot, as we try to keep them apart, but again I fear it may already be too late.

"You need some rest," Gibby tells me.

We have stopped taking turns at our son's side, and are now together beside our little boy, because he does not seem to be getting any better. I have been keeping the baby away as much as possible, which is a terribly difficult task as the baby needs to be fed, and there is not enough time to attend to a newborn and a sick child. I am either nursing a newborn or wiping my son down to try to break his fever. There is no time to sleep as there is always something or someone needing attending to. I do my best with what I have, and hope it is enough.

"So do you, and I am not leaving his side," I whisper to my husband, trying not to disturb my sleeping son.

It's only March, and there aren't many farming chores to be done, so Gibby and I can thankfully spend almost all of our time at our son's side. In the dead of night, with only a small glow from the lamp, Earl stirs and opens his eyes. I look into my little boy's face, but he seems to be looking through me. The doctor stopped by yesterday and said that if he does not improve soon, we'd probably lose him. He told us to continue trying to break his fever the way we've been doing, and pray. We have been doing both fervently.

"Earl, would you like some water?" I ask him. He looks at me listlessly, exhausted from his fever and the wracking cough that tortures him. He closes his eyes, and I see his breathing slow. This is dreadful to watch, as we can do nothing to help him. His labored breathing goes on for hours, while we continually wipe him down. I sing the songs I sang to him when he was a newborn, and stroke his damp face.

Even with all our tending and love, he does not open his eyes again. Sometime before morning he shudders once, and I know he is gone from us. I see his little chest lie still, and I cannot believe that last night was the last time I will see my little boy's eyes. Gibby looks at me in shock and I am sure I look the same to him.

I start to sob quietly, as I do not want to wake the other children, and I certainly don't want to scare Bert. He is laying on a cot across the room, and I don't want to wake him as he needs his rest to fight this illness.

Gibby pulls the sheet over Earl's head, and we both bow our heads in prayer. My body shakes with the effort of trying to cry silently, to keep this horror from Bert.

My streak of luck in not losing a child to diphtheria has been broken, and I am broken as well.

Monday, March 9th, 1885

There has been no time to mourn my deceased son, as Bert is just as ill now.

How can this be? Am I to lose both sons? My firstborns? My twins? It does not even seem possible to lose one, never mind both. But I cannot even think these thoughts right now, as Bert is coughing in the same horrific way Earl once did.

I cannot mourn, as I must be strong and try to save my surviving son. Gibby and I are frantic, continually wiping him down with wet cloths and trying to break his fever. I have applied the same poultice to his chest, hoping it will soak in and help him to breathe. I sing the same songs I sang to Earl, I do everything I did for his brother, only this time with more desperation as I know what the result will be if I do not succeed.

We have gotten him to drink some broth, but all of this to no avail. One has to be very careful what you feed a diphtheria patient as they can choke to death very easily. Many victims have dreadfully swollen throats, some so swollen their neck appears broken.

Gibby and I tend to the girls when we can, and they are little angels at this time. It's as if they know they have to behave as we cannot give them the attention they deserve. Baby Charles is the same. I am so grateful he is content to just eat and sleep, as I have no time or patience to deal with a fussy baby.

The tension in the house is palpable. Everyone feels it. We go on for a few days like this, the house silent, almost as if it also knows there is a life teetering precariously on the brink.

Then Bert wakes one morning and seems a lot better. He asks me how Earl is, and I don't have the heart to tell him yet. He assumes we are keeping them apart due to the illness, and he is too exhausted to ask us where his brother has gone.

"Spring will be here soon. You know how you love the warm summer days that are coming," I tell my remaining twin son. Smiling at him as if my heart is not broken. I hope I am playing my part well. I don't want to cause him any worry.

"Yes Mama, I hope I'll feel better soon" he says to me. I look at him and I'm hopeful. Today he doesn't seem to feel as warm, although his throat is more swollen than his brother's ever was. But I don't want to worry right now, I just want to hang on to something good, and the good is that he is awake and talking, and it looks like his fever has broken.

Gibby and I spend the evening at his side, as we've been doing for the last week.

Our friends and other townsfolk have been incredibly kind. They have been helping with taking care of our animals, and drop food off to our family. I'm always surprised and grateful when Gibby brings in a basket of food left by our front door. There is no time to cook between caring for a sick child, a newborn and two other little ones.

The generosity and thoughtfulness of our little town lift my spirits.

Surely we cannot possibly lose both twins to this sickness.

Can we?

Wednesday, March 11th, 1885

It seems we can indeed lose both boys, as Bert has now joined his brother in endless sleep.

Gibby and I watched him take his last breath early this morning, and we are both in deep shock.

How can one family lose both their sons? How is this possible? I just want to lie in my bed and cry. But the circle of life travels on, and my newborn baby and two young daughters need to be taken care of. They are too young to understand what is going on, blessedly. I wish it were the same for Gibby and me.

Sleep eludes me, and I sit most of the night in my parlor chair in the dark. The dark is comforting. At some point I know I will have to get some rest, as my children need me. As does Gibby. He has lost both of his sons, his little companions, and more lately his helpers. He walks around in a daze, and I wonder if I have that same look about me too. That blank look of despair. I feel as though the corners of my mouth have weights, pulling my cheeks down, and it feels truly impossible that my cheeks will ever rise into a smile.

The moonlight streams into my parlor, casting long shadows across the room. My chair is not far from the window, and in the faint moonlight, I can see my newborn son's peaceful face. I know he and my daughters are why I must contain my grief. Why I must go on. It is almost as if my children know how much I need them. Mary Alice tries to help me, and has hugged me so many times today. There is nothing like a hug from a little one, and I sorely need them now.

The undertaker will pick up the boys this morning, as they are to go to a vault until we are ready for burial. I do not think I will ever be ready. There will be no wake because of worries that the illness will spread.

It does not seem possible this is happening to us.

But sadly it is.

Monday, May 4th, 1885

The exceptionally cold winter has caused a delay in burying the twins, and I am grateful they are in a vault as we wait for the ground to thaw out, so I do not have to think of them lying lifeless on our property. My mind is active enough with its morbid thoughts, and knowing they are somewhere I cannot imagine and have not visited, helps me calm myself.

Their deaths made us do something we'd never even given thought to, which is to find a place to bury them. There are a few cemeteries in town, but seeing as we own a lot of acreage Gibby has picked a place in the middle of our fields.

This spot is located up the hill from the spring the boys used to walk to together. Where they ran happily about in the field. They will now lie in rest where they played and scampered, something that I fervently hope would have pleased them

While I struggle to go about my everyday tasks, Gibby has been toiling with the help of Jasper and Everett, to build a stone wall that surrounds their resting place, so it will be more of an official cemetery.

It is a parent's worst horror come true. To have to prepare to bury their child, or in our case children.

With their quick work, the little rectangular cemetery soon lies ready for its first inhabitants, which I fervently wish were Gibby and me rather than two wonderful, active little boys, both sadly only six years of age.

The dreaded day finally comes when the earth is warm enough to dig the graves.

While the men take care of this depressing task, I wait within my home with my beloved friends Cora and Delphine, who are both as speechless with grief as I am. They knew my sons well, and it is close to home for them. They both saw them arrive into this world, never thinking they would leave it before us.

No one wants to see anyone near them lose a child. Especially from something so easily caught as diphtheria.

As Delphine brushes my hair, she hums a hymn I don't recognize, but enjoy all the same. It is a soothing sound. My friends have not said much to me, and I do not expect them to.

What can anyone say at a time like this?

Especially people who have not lost a child, and do not know how much my heart and body aches. How I cry all night, wake, and weep again. It's as though my sorrow has no end, and overwhelms me all the time. I am grateful for moments like this when the grief abates, when I can just sit quietly with no feeling.

Delphine continues to brush my hair, relaxing me. She will put it in a bun for the ceremony. There is a little fire going in both the kitchen and the parlor as we try to take the chill out of the home. Charles is as always at my breast, and I listen to the crackle of the fire, which is soothing.

As we waited for the ground to thaw, I made a black mourning dress and Cora is now getting it ready for me.

I sit, thankful that I have no more decisions to make, knowing my friends can be trusted to do whatever I require. It is a relief for me to be so well taken care of.

Apart from the crackle of the fire, it is quiet in my home, the grief of our loss enveloping everything and everyone in its path, like a heavy wet blanket that may never dry.

My house is also silent from the cries of two loud little boys who could never come into a room quietly. They stomped about, ran about, but always were open to a hug from Mama or Papa. They had small, perfectly formed hands that would proudly bring me flowers picked from the fields where they will now lay.

Now it will be me delivering them flowers for as long as I am able to.

There is a light knock, and the door to my home opens, and it is Everett who eventually appears at my bedroom entrance, where we all are waiting.

"It's time Mercy, Gibby sent me as he needed to stay behind to finish," he tells me quietly, from his place at the door frame. I imagine Gibby is overcome and wants some time to gather himself before we all arrive. When we are alone we hold each other tight in our grief, and I am sure he is struggling with the knowledge that he has just finished digging graves for two of his children.

"Thank you, Everett" I reply, and I pick up my straw hat, which will remain plain today without no decoration but a single black ribbon. This is for the most somber of occasions I will ever have the misfortune of attending. My friend Delphine has placed the black ribbon around the hat to match my mourning dress, and with any luck I shall never wear it again.

Delphine takes Charles from my arms, and then loops her other arm through mine, as Cora does the same at my other side. It's as though they work together in their task of comforting me, readying me for the dismal walk to the graveyard. I am grateful to be guided and led, and not asked to make any decisions.

Everett rounds up the children, who follow like a row of somber ducks, heads bowed as they absorb the melancholy around them. They're thankfully too young to understand the full meaning of this occasion.

Our somber group trudges from the back of our home into my yard, where the day is cool and cloudy. I rejoice for that at least. As I always say, the day should not be warm, sunny and happy when you are settling a loved one into their perpetual rest, especially my beloved twins.

We walk across Hell Hollow Road, following the familiar path I took so often with the boys. The path as always leads by the woods, past the spring and into the field.

We silently follow the tracks of the wheels of the hearse wagon. These tracks and the men's footsteps have left us a muddy path to follow. My friends still flank me, propelling me forward to something I never dreamed I would have to do. This path will end with me standing at the grave of not one of my children, but two.

Has anyone ever been so tormented?

Or cursed? At this point, it seems not.

We finally reach the new little cemetery, the fresh stones stacked in perfect lines to form a rectangle. No moss or lichen is on these stones, as they have been freshly removed from somewhere to mark the boundaries of this godforsaken place. I am still in disbelief this brand new cemetery is for my own family.

As we arrive, I notice there are other people in the small cemetery, and I try to nod my head at them to acknowledge them but struggle to even do this. Now I know exactly how many of them felt at the burials of their own family members. I see Louise on the outskirts of the group, supporting me as I once supported her. I look at her, and she looks back and offers a slight nod. It's barely noticeable, but I see it. I know she is aware of just how I am feeling.

Walking slowly, I see that everyone attending is dressed like me, in black. It is a somber occasion indeed.

While I am absorbing all of this, Gibby arrives at my side, and Cora lets him take my arm, placing a hand on my back to give me strength through her touch. I see now there are two gaping holes, with twin coffins lying nearby, and our pastor standing at the head of them.

Is this real? I want to pinch myself to see if I am dreaming. Surely this horrible scene is not for me? I look to my husband to reassure myself, and I see his strong profile, looking ahead as a single tear runs down his cheek. There is my answer. This is not a nightmare I would love to awaken from with two healthy boys by my side. I have never seen my husband cry, and I hope this is the last time I witness it. I turn my gaze back to the coffins in front of me, and we stop in front of them.

The pastor nods his head to me now that I have arrived, and starts to speak. I see his mouth move and know he is talking but it is as if I am in a tunnel, void of any sound. Honestly, what words could be said to comfort me, or Gibby at this time? A slight wind sighs through the field that chills my face like a cold slap. But I also feel the touch of Delphine, Cora, and Gibby, which gives me warmth like a ray of sunshine appearing after a rainstorm.

The ceremony is short, and I cannot tell you much about it, as I don't know how I even managed to stand and stay upright through it all. All at once, I hear my loved ones saying "Amen" and I mouth the word silently as well. Not consciously, but from memory and habit.

Cora's boys are walking over to me, and I stare at them, bewildered, as they hand me small bouquets they have picked. I am disappointed in myself that I have not done this task of picking flowers to place on my sons' caskets. Feeling guilty, I muster a small smile at them and take the little bouquets.

I disengage myself from everyone holding me and walk to the little coffins. Standing in between them, I place a bouquet on each, then spread my hands to touch them. I feel the soft, smooth cool wood under my hands, the smell the new timber reminding me of the toy chest in their bedroom. I remember when Gibby and I bought it and enjoyed the smell of new wood. But this is not a moment for pride or happiness. Everything is desolation. The new wood of these coffins will take my boys from me forever, into the ground.

I stand like this for a moment, knowing that this is the closest I will ever be to my little boys again, and I am silent. Tears run down my face as I start to cry, and then my three living angels come forward and take my hands to guide me away. My husband gives me a hug, and then offers a hand to Delphine, and then one to Cora. Cora is now holding Charles, and I am glad that he is in good hands. Gibby nods at my friends, and they pull my hands to the crooks of each of their arms to comfort me as they walk closer to my side. We are three abreast, with me in the center, as they gently walk me forward, out of the field and away from my boys.

I do not look back. I do not turn my head, but instead I look forward toward my home. I know that behind me, the men are lowering those little wooden coffins into the ground then anchoring them in the holes with soil, planting them forever.

This is something I do not wish to see, could not bear to see, and I am grateful I am not having to witness it. I used to think women were the stronger sex, but now I feel that may be wrong. I think both sexes are strong, and that there are some things Gibby cannot do, and some I cannot. And I could not lower those coffins into the cool damp earth. I can't even watch as my husband does so.

The walk back seems quicker, and I soon arrive at my home with Cora and Delphine. They sit me in my chair in the parlor with my youngest child, and prepare to feed whoever wants to eat after this somber occasion. Baby Charles is sleeping in my arms, and stays there through this horrible day. He will never know the laughter of his brothers, or see their round little faces with tall cowlicks on their foreheads. He will never play with them, wrestle with them or know their love. I watch him contentedly sleeping and think it may perhaps be a good thing that he does not know what he has lost.

The ladies know I have not eaten or slept in a few days, and they are now in the parlor pressuring me to eat. I relent and have some warm soup that slides down my throat, warming me from the inside out. How I can be alive to enjoy soup while my children lie in a cold grave, I wonder.

I now understand the grief others have been through in this town, and wonder how they survive it. It is an inspiration to me, just knowing that they carry on with their daily tasks, and I have actually seen many of them smile again. Sometimes seeing other people survive something is what presses people on. What gives them strength? I know I will be looking to them for guidance to survive this deep loss.

A little later the rear door of our home opens, and the men return, their shoulders slumped, and their faces drawn. The ladies get food for them, as I am not able to do much of anything. Gibby comes to my side, and I stand with Charles in front of him, and he takes me into his arms and I sob.

Wednesday. July 1st, 1885

More than a few months have passed since the death of my boys. Months of sadness and many tear-filled days. Mary Alice is old enough to realize that her brothers are gone, and she is sad sometimes as well. But Maud Ella is too young and has already stopped asking about them.

What an awful thing it is to forget, and to forget so quickly. I vow to never forget my boys and work hard to have everyone else remember them.

I finally have the courage to visit their little graves early one summer day. I walk along the path leading me to the spring and onward to our new cemetery.

Standing within the walls of the little cemetery, I see that the ground has healed itself, with fresh grass growing. One might think it is just a grassy area except for the bright white cross impaling the ground with the names "Bert and Earl, 1885" on it. I know without looking, the other side has "Reynolds."

Their grave does not look so fresh now. I don't feel the same on the inside, either. I feel as though my insides have been torn asunder, and they ache. Oh, how I ache.

Gibby and I clutch each other at night, in our little bed, hoping we can give each other strength. I find it strange that life goes on so easily after such heartbreak. How can everyone go about their everyday tasks when I am so broken inside? Perhaps this is a good thing, as these everyday tasks continue to propel me forward.

Every day that passes makes me a little stronger.

I spend a few moments, then I leave our little cemetery, and walk back along the path I now know so well.

Back in our home I head to our kitchen to the ever-faithful cookbook to find a recipe. There is a large picnic planned in town for Independence Day, which we are planning to attend. I am looking for something to bring, and cannot bring myself to make the twins' favorite royal ham sandwiches. It just doesn't seem right to be enjoying one of their favorite meals without them.

I finally come across a recipe for chicken sandwiches. They also travel easily, and we never ate them with the boys. This little thought brings me comfort. I now do enough things without them, so eating something new and something we have not experienced with them is a good thing. I try hard to find happiness in the smallest things these days.

Charles is another well-tempered baby, and I rejoice that I still have three healthy children and hope with all my heart this always remains so. But I know death comes easily, and the knowledge frightens me. Perhaps losing two children already means I have paid enough. Perhaps I will be safe from sorrow now. I know in my heart that nothing is promised, but I can only hope I that I have had my share of sorrow in this life, and that I do not lose any more of my children.

I can only hope.

Saturday, July 4th, 1885

It is the annual Independence Day picnic in our town, something the boys and I used to look forward to very much. Some days I feel as though I am just going through the motions, and perform my chores in a daze. Today is a day I feel their presence strongly, as they would have been so excited to travel to town and see their friends and the fireworks after. The children are all in the parlor waiting as I get ready to depart.

Charles is now six months old and a happy baby. He smiles his toothless grin at anyone who looks at him, bringing a smile to our faces. Mary Alice is five but seems older, since she has already experienced so much, and Maud Ella turned two in May. Time is traveling along as it always does with or without our loved ones beside us.

Time stands still for no one.

With Aunt Babette's help, I have made a chicken salad that I shall spread on homemade bread for us to eat, and I have pickles made from last year's garden and a batch of vanilla cookies for dessert. It's nice to have a few extra cookies to share with others as well.

I am in the middle of gathering the items we will need for our outing today when I hear the back door shut and footsteps heading to my kitchen. Gibby appears in the doorway. He is dressed in his standard trousers with dark suspenders, with a white short-sleeved shirt underneath, and he smiles at me, making his beard do its typical jiggle.

"What time would you like to leave for the picnic? The O'Dowds have already passed by on their way." He tells me.

"I'm just packing what we need, so if you want to harness Smokey and pull the wagon up, I'll be ready," I tell him. He leaves the kitchen and again I hear the door shut as he goes outside.

I have wrapped the sandwiches in some paper, and the pickles will stay safely in their jar to travel. The cookies are in a tin, and I am adding some napkins as well as some lemonade that has been chilling in my ice box since last night. The lemonade will no doubt warm up a little as we travel there, but I am hopeful it might still be refreshing on this hot summer day. Packing these items into my picnic basket, I place a cloth around the bottles to insulate them for a while, and to also catch the dampness from them so our sandwiches don't get soggy.

My packing is complete, and I close the basket and place it by the door, knowing Gibby will come back to help me with the basket and the children. I add a blanket from the hall closet for us to sit on, then walk to the parlor to check on the children.

As I expected, they are playing together nicely. Charles is lying on a blanket, kicking and grabbing his feet, while Maud Ella and Mary Alice are stacking blocks. As I enter the room they look up at me and smile, and I return their smile.

"Let's pick those blocks up so we can leave for the picnic. Would you like to bring them to play with?" I ask Mary Alice.

"No Mama, I will play with Aurore and Alecia when we get there," she says, already starting to pick the blocks up and place them in their bag as she was asked.

Poor Mary Alice, now the eldest, and so serious already. She is young, but so helpful with the little ones, and I want to see her smiling happily along with the other children. I hope today she has some fun and takes some enjoyment from playing with her little friends. Bending over, I help her with her task as Maud Ella hands me a block as well.

Maud Ella's hair has darkened a little to brown, and she has hazel eyes, which seems to be a Reynolds trait. She is even-tempered, as all my children are. After she sees me put her block in the sack, she raises her hands to be picked up, and I oblige. There is a lot to be said about holding a little one when your heart is hurting. She clings to me, as I hear Gibby come back into the house to join us.

"Could you please pick up little Charles for me?" I ask him, as I do not want to put Maud Ella down so soon. He doesn't answer, but walks to the baby who has rolled over onto his stomach and is now fretting, as he doesn't seem to care for his new position. Gibby picks him up and holds him in the crook of his arm.

I remember I'll need some rags for the babes in case they need to be changed, and I go into the children's room to their bureau, and pull a drawer open to gather some for our trip.

I peek into Maud Ella's diaper to see if she needs changing, but she is still clean and dry. I gather a good amount of folded diapers from the wardrobe drawer, close it, and then return to the parlor.

"I'm ready" I call out as I walk to the door and place the clothes on top of the picnic basket. Gibby picks the basket up and we walk out the door with Mary Alice following us and load ourselves into our wagon.

Glancing at my children sitting in the back, and the hard bench Gibby and I are sitting on, makes me think of the lovely carriage that my parents travel in. I hope one day we can afford a carriage like that, as it would be lovely to travel comfortably rather than in a bouncy long wagon. Gibby taps the reins onto Smokey's back and we are on our way.

We arrive a little late to the celebration by the river, and we're lucky to find a place to leave our wagon. There are horses, oxen and wagons everywhere, as it is a popular picnic that people look forward to all year. I know my boys certainly did, and as usual the thought of them saddens me. I look around at my surroundings, to get the desolate thoughts out of my mind. I sense Gibby at my side, waiting to help baby Charles and me down.

Once we are all on the ground, Maud Ella instantly comes to my side and places her little hand in mine. I smile down at her happy little face, and we walk together toward all the people gathered in the field, with Mary Alice trailing behind.

It saddens me she is alone and not in the shadows of her older brothers, all of them laughing and happy. Gibby seems to notice this as well, and he slows his pace to walk with his daughter. As we walk, we spot the Culvers and O'Dowds already sitting together. Thankfully they have saved a spot for us latecomers. I smile and walk a bit faster, anxious to see my friends and shake the sadness from myself. We reach them at last, and Gibby sets the basket down. He unfolds the blanket, shaking it out to lie flat upon the ground. Once the blanket finds its place, we find our own place to sit. I find myself at the edge closest to my friends who are already eating their food.

"I didn't realize we were that late!" I say with a smile.

"You are only a bit late, it's just that we are so hungry!" Delphine says, taking a bite from what she is eating.

I turn to my basket and start to take out my paper bundles, the jars of pickles and the cookies, along with napkins. The girls wait for their paper-wrapped sandwiches along with Gibby. Once everyone has their food and the lemonade has been poured into some small glasses, I take out my own food and start to eat as well. I am always the last to eat in our family, as I have to be certain my family is served first.

The sun beats down on us in the open field, and the heat surrounds all the picnickers. It is a typical hot July day, although it's a bit humid and the air hangs thick and heavy. The adults talk quietly while eating their meals, and the children do the same.

"Did you hear the Statue of Liberty has finally arrived on our shores?' Gibby asks Everett.

"I did hear the news. She arrived in June. I'd love to see how they are going to put her together. It will be quite a feat. They say she's very tall and she'll be a wondrous sight for ships sailing into New York harbor," Everett says.

"I imagine she'll be quite a welcome sight for those coming across the sea to our country," I remark, thinking how much I would love to see her myself one day.

We finish our picnic food and continue chatting idly when a woman and her boys walk to us.

"Hello, Mercy. I am Matilda Hopkins, and these are my boys Ebenezer and Alfred," she says to me. She is a petite blonde woman, with her hair pulled back in a bun like mine. Her eyes are blue and kind. Her boys are blond like her, but with honey-brown eyes. I notice one is taller than the other, but they are close in age to what my boys would have been.

"Hello Matilda, it's a pleasure to meet you" I reply to her. Her boys stand close to her skirts, looking nervous.

"My sons went to school with yours, and I just wanted to say how sorry I am for your loss. I lost a daughter to diphtheria last year. I understand and I just wanted to tell you that I share your sorrow." She gives me a timid smile, while her boys continue to cling to her skirts.

"Thank you very much, Matilda, I'm sorry for your loss as well." She smiles sadly at me then turns away to return to her family.

I sit in silence for a minute, grateful I am not alone in my sorrow, and then instantly feel bad for Matilda that she is suffering as I am. Mary Alice comes from behind me and drapes her arms around my neck, enveloping me in an embrace to comfort me. Reaching my arms up, I clutch her arms in return and we stay in this position until some shouting breaks the moment. Looking, we see a baseball game has formed, and Jasper is walking toward them to play as well. Gibby has stayed behind, as he is much older and would rather relax and watch, rather than take part. We are in a great position to watch the activity from our blankets, so we sit and relax and enjoy the game.

The afternoon flies by, and before long it is dusk. We watch the men light the fire and prepare to set off the fireworks. I sit on my blanket with my children around me and sigh. Their little hands are clasped within my own, and I enjoy the way they fit against mine.

I do not take these moments for granted, as who can know any of our futures? I would never have dreamt the twins would be missing from this annual event, but here we are, without them. That is the thing with loss. You continually think about the missing souls, even at the oddest times. But no matter what, they are still gone. Vanished. Like the seeds of a dandelion that ride on the wind then disappear.

As always, I am grateful for my other children, as their presence and dependency upon me help me to move on.

We sit together, huddled, illuminated by changing colors as the fireworks burst above us.

Then all at once the loud noises and bright colors that Charles did not enjoy are done, and we are picking up our blanket and remnants of dinner and heading home.

Monday, September 7th, 1885

There is a lot of talk in town about today being a new holiday called Labor Day. They have been trying to create a holiday, a day off to celebrate labor workers for a few years now. Many towns have created laws to celebrate it, and word has spread quickly. With so many people toiling every day, it is a pleasure indeed to have an extra day of rest.

Although we are not really part of the workforce, Gibby is still taking a day off from working in the fields to spend with us today. We plan on passing some time by the river in town, with some of the other families.

It will be nice to do something new to take our minds off our loss. Hopefully, this will become an official holiday that we can all enjoy. Time will tell, but for now, we enjoy the day together.

Wednesday, September 30th, 1885

It is fall again in our little hollow. The landscape has taken a lovely golden tint, and the sky is a bright cerulean blue, making for a colorful landscape. We are all trying to fill the hole the twins have left. We miss their antics and their smiling little faces.

Charlie is starting to sit up and he'll be crawling soon. His little toothless smile makes us smile in return through our sadness. Mary Alice and Maud Ella are also happy little girls, and these giggly children are certainly helping to heal our broken hearts.

It is harvest time, and Jasper is helping Gibby with our harvest, a favor Gibby will return at their farm. Cora has had another child, a girl this time, so they now have three.

My twins lie sleeping beneath the grass in the beautiful field across from our home, and I have gotten into a routine of visiting them every week.

Each Saturday, after our breakfast, we head out our front door, walk across the road and follow the well-worn path to our family cemetery.

We walk along the shaded trail bordering a field of tall grass with flowers sprinkled in between. The trail eventually leaves the comfort of the shade and turns up the hill into the field, and at this point we all pick a few flowers to place upon their graves. While I hold Charlie, the girls run about collecting flowers in the field for their bouquets. Bees fly from flower to flower, the sun shines down, and a light breeze moves the grass and the girls' hair. I pause and just raise my face to the sky.

A tug on my skirt breaks the moment, and I look down into Mary Alice's round little face. She raises her arm upwards and shows me a little fist full of daisies and some other type of purple flower. I smile at her, and she smiles back.

"Flowers for the twins," she says looking anxiously at my face.

"Yes, flowers for the twins. I am sure they are looking down and I'm just as sure they're grateful that you're thinking of them." I say this with a little catch in my throat. I thought it might get easier as time went on. But I find that although I may not cry as often, the loss is always there. It's like a heavy anchor dragging behind me. I have to learn to live with this weight that never leaves, and sometimes it gets snagged on something and pulls me down all over again.

But today I look into my little daughter's face and see she is trying so hard to bring me a little happiness. I must be strong for her. Perhaps this is how people move on… for the sake of others. I smile at her, and she smiles in return.

"Let's go leave them for the twins, and then get back to make some cookies," I tell Mary Alice.

"Yes, Mama," she says. We turn and continue up the field to the little rectangle of stones that holds our two precious loved ones within.

We make it there in no time at all, opening the little white gate between the stone walls and walking inside. I shut it after me and continue towards the white cross which always stands out crisp and clean against the grass.

When I reach it, I sink to my knees, with Charlie still in my arms, and place my free hand upon the cross, bowing my head. I remain like this for a moment, and then feel Mary Alice beside me. She places her bouquet carefully at the base of the cross, then puts her arm around my shoulder and tilts her head to mine. Maud Ella, still very young, walks to my other side and leans into me. We pause like this for a minute, in the warm sun. There is no sound, just a light breeze ticking the hair at the side of my face. We are a family missing our loved ones.

I enjoy the closeness of my children for a few moments, then lean over and give each girl a kiss on their cheek, and stand.

It is my fervent hope there will be no other inhabitants at our little cemetery for a very long time.

Walking away from the cross, we open the gate again and close it behind us as we pass out of our little family cemetery. We walk back down the hill, on through the shade of the covered trail, to our home that waits patiently for us.

Monday, December 28th, 1885

Christmas has come and gone, this one a bit more solemn due to the absence of two boisterous little boys. We remember the antics last year, getting the tree and sledding down from the knoll. We manage, and the girls enjoy their new dolls and dresses. Charles has a new teddy, and over the years we have amassed a few toys, so the children have lots to entertain them through the dreary cold months of winter.

My mother has kindly sent me some of her silverware, and I will finally have enough utensils for when I entertain. The bonus is that they were my Grandma Antonia's. I think of her whenever I use them and plan on making sure my children know about her. I believe we should talk of our family that has passed, as they live on this way.

I have to say that I am not able to speak much about my boys yet. The wound is still too fresh. But I hope that one day I can tell my other children all about them, so they live on through their siblings. Time will tell if I can do this.

Snow covers the ground on this winter day, and our family is all outside with Smokey hitched to our wagon as we prepare to take a ride to the Culvers. We are meeting them for our annual sleigh ride, which the twins loved, and now the girls are starting to enjoy it as well.

We settle into the wagon and start on our way, the large wagon wheels easily making their way through the freshly fallen snow.

The landscape is pretty, and the white blanket of snow makes everything look clean and fresh. The houses we pass have white covered roofs and the usual ribbon of smoke from their fireplaces winding into the sky.

Hell Hollow Road is a bit difficult to pass in spots, but once we reach Ekonk Hill, the wagon rolls along easily enough. While we are out we will also make our typical visits to Whitford's for a few things we need.

We roll past farms, homesteads, and open snow-covered fields before finally arriving at the Culvers' home. Gibby guides Smokey into the yard and stops him behind the house. Once down from the wagon, we walk to the back door of their farmhouse.

Gibby raps his knuckles on the door, and Delphine answers with a large smile and a protruding belly. She is once again with child. I guide my daughters inside and embrace my friend. I release her and help the girls with their shoes, which are covered in snow. Once the shoes are removed, they run off to join the Culver girls.

The fireplace welcomes us with its flames and warmth. I settle in with the children, but Gibby keeps his coat on, since he and Everett are going to Whitford's for necessities, while we ladies visit. Once they return we'll all take off in the sleigh. The men take the lists we have made, and head out into the snow to procure the items.

Happy to be staying behind, Delphine and I head into the parlor, where the girls are already playing, and seat ourselves on the chairs in front of the fire.

"How are you feeling?" I ask Delphine, nodding at her belly.

"Very well, all things considered. I am hoping my lying in is like yours. Oh to be so lucky," she says with a large smile.

"I hope so too," I reply. If the weather cooperates I will be attending her lying in, just as I did with her daughters. It is comforting to have a good friend present when giving birth. And who better to attend a woman in labor than a woman who has her own experience of giving birth? We are all midwives, in a sense, helping each other.

We talk about the schools in town, and a local family that needs some help, and we pass the time this way till our husbands' return. The men arrive with their shopping, along with a little brown bag for each of the girls. The girls are already learning what the little bag is … a bag of delights. Charlie is still too young to enjoy the sweets, but the girls look into their bags and before we know it they are already eating.

"Girls, these are meant for the sleigh ride!" Gibby exclaims, smiling under his bushy beard.

The girls close their bags but continue to chew on the candy they have already managed to cram into their mouths.

With the men returned, we gather our coats and blankets and head outside to the waiting sleigh. Gibby and Everett help Delphine and me in first, then Gibby hands Charlie to me, and the girls climb up beside us. We wrap the blankets around ourselves and wait for the men to take their places at the front. Once they do, Everett clicks his tongue at the horses, and we are off.

The sleigh sighs as it travels smoothly over the snow, with the dull clopping of the horse's hooves joining in. The jingling of the horse's harness adds a festive mood as we glide along. The bells are still enjoyable even though Christmas has passed. I look at the four girls and they all have broad smiles as they enjoy their ride.

Everett takes us down the hill, over the bridge and we turn into the field where we have the Independence Day celebrations. People are now ice skating on the frozen pond, and it is a lovely sight. We stop and watch them for a while, then Everett lightly taps the reins on the horses' backs, and we are off again up the hill and out onto the main road.

This time Everett takes a right onto Providence Road, and we travel along past more houses all emitting that same smoke ribbon from well-banked fireplaces. The snow covers everything we can see and seems to muffle all sound. At the end of Providence Road we stop, and to our right is a round stone wall with a gate, which is our animal pound, where lost animals are brought for the owner to find them. It is empty at this time of year, but throughout the summer it can hold quite a few escaped beasts waiting for their owners to find them and take them home.

Everett turns left and we are off again, this time headed to the little town of Moosup. We come down the hill with a large mill on our right, the largest in our town. It is called the Sterling Manufacturing Company, and it produces lots of cloth for the south. They do not have the kind of mills we have in the south, so the raw cotton is brought up here to these mills to be woven into fabric. The workers are mostly French Canadians who have emigrated here from Canada to work and live. Many children work here too, young children working in dangerous conditions. As always, I am grateful we are farmers and my children will not be working there at all, although they may when they are adults, as there are not a lot of options for employment besides the mills.

We travel on and finally reach the village of Almyville, home to the Almyville Mill, with lots of mill houses running along the long straight street. Onward we travel, passing a few wagons and other sleighs with passengers waving happily to us as we fly past.

We reach downtown Moosup, which is a pretty little town, with a row of brick buildings with awnings hanging out over the street. Shop owners bundled up from the cold are outside clearing the sidewalks, and I look at the shop windows as we pass by.

I always enjoy looking at shop windows, to see what the shop owner has displayed in the hopes that someone will buy what he is displaying. We pass a pharmacy, a bakery, a stable, and some other little shops while enjoying our ride. Onward we travel, passing yet another mill, this one named the Majestic.

We turn onto a bridge and over Moosup River, heading back to our original starting point. Now the views are no longer of towns and mills. Now we're back among homesteads, farms and open fields. Before we know it we are pulling back into the Culvers after a delightful sleigh ride.

The girls were at first chatty, enjoying their little bags of treats, but by the time we arrive at the Culvers' they are slumped against us, soothed to sleep by the steady rhythm of the horse's hooves and the smooth glide of the sleigh. The sleigh comes to a halt, and the motion stirs the girls, who blink in wonder they have returned home.

Everett and Gibby climb down, then help the rest of us out of the sleigh and onto the ground. By this time it is late afternoon, and we say our goodbyes to the Culver's and pile back into our wagon to return to our own home.

It is afternoons like this that nourish my aching heart. Good times spent with friends, watching our remaining children smiling happily.

Tuesday, February 2nd, 1886

We are sitting in our respective chairs in front of a fire with the dark night surrounding us. There is a little glow from a kerosene lamp as well as the fire, but the windows are black as ink, and the night outside the walls of our home is dark and cold.

The children are asleep and Gibby and I are relaxing, when we suddenly hear the sound of a horse and wagon entering our yard. Gibby goes to the rear of our home to see who it is at this time of the night. It is Everett, and I already know why he has come. I run into my room and grab what I will need to attend to Delphine for her lying in. Luckily Everett has brought his wagon, as I am no horsewoman like his own Delphine. I reach the door at the same time he knocks, and I let him into our home.

"Evening Gibby, I've come to fetch Mercy. Delphine's time has arrived," Everett tells us, breathless from his hurried journey.

"I'm ready," I tell him, as I am sure there is no time to waste. I kiss Gibby on the cheek and follow Everett to his waiting wagon. His horse paws at the ground, anxious to get back to his warm stall, just as we are anxious to get to Delphine. Everett helps me up into the wagon, then he runs to his own side, and as soon as he sits down, he flicks the reins to get his horse going. The horse takes off like a shot, and we are on our way, out of our yard and up the hill from the hollow.

We arrive in good time, and as we enter their home, I see Delphine is pacing the floor in her kitchen. I set my bag down, and run to her side.

"How are you faring, my friend?" I ask of her.

"My waters have broken, and my pains are only a few minutes apart," she answers. Everett's mother appears. Delphine's mother lives in New York and won't get here until after the birth to see her new grandchild.

"Your room is waiting, Delphine," says Nanny, who then turns to me. "Hello Mercy, I'm glad you made it," she says. It is always nice to have two people at a birth to help and to also be there for support in case anything goes awry. Lying ins can be tricky, and do not always have a jubilant conclusion.

"I am glad to be here as well," I tell Nanny with a smile. Delphine's **mother in law** is a tall, thin woman with a clear complexion and beautiful features. It is perhaps the kindness she exudes that makes her such a beautiful woman. She loves her daughter-in-law immensely, and I have always thought Delphine very lucky indeed to have such a mother-in-law. Nanny lives in the neighboring town of Canterbury but has been staying with Delphine and Everett the last few days, knowing her time was close.

I retrieve my bag and join Nanny and help Delphine to her room. The room has a lamp glowing and clean sheets on the bed, and a water basin and some clothes on the night table. A fire glows and crackles in the fireplace. The room is warm and inviting. It's a lovely place to welcome a baby to the world.

Delphine continues to pace, but now she is in her room, and the walk is shorter, more of a back and forth. I set my bag down on a chair, along with my coat, and then join her side to pace with her.

"Have you decided on any names yet, Delphine?" I ask to distract her from her pains. Sometimes a bit of distraction is very welcome to laboring mothers.

"Evaline for a girl, and Everett for a boy," Delphine replies.

The Culvers adore their girls, but I know that no matter what sex they have, they will be very happy. All they want is a healthy baby. Isn't that true for most parents?

"Those are lovely names," I tell her, continuing to walk alongside her.

Nanny brings a pitcher of water into the room, along with a few glasses.

"No water for me please," Delphine tells Nanny. Nanny sets the glasses and pitcher on the bedside table, and then sits in a chair on the side of the room to wait.

Delphine and I pace together for a few hours, knowing the walking will help the babe come out faster. All at once, Delphine doubles over in pain, and I tell her it is time to get into her bed. She obeys and sits herself in the middle of the bed.

I stoke the fire to make sure the room is nice and warm, while Nanny pours some water onto a cloth for Delphine's forehead.

Delphine holds our hands as she labors for a while, and then all at once, she tells us she feels the need to push. We help her pull up her nightdress, and she assumes the position women since early times have done to give birth. Sitting with legs wide open, she looks so vulnerable! Once Delphine is in place, I lift her long night dress, to see how she is progressing, and already I can see the head.

"Delphine, you are really close!" I exclaim while Nanny presses the cloth to Delphine's forehead. Delphine bears down again to push, but there is no movement forward as yet. I worry a bit, but I know it usually takes more than one push to expel a baby from a laboring mother. We also have some cooking grease on hand to help ease the baby out if needs be.

Delphine is panting, and mustering strength for another push, and this goes on for about a half-hour. The room has become hot and stuffy, and Delphine's hair is stuck to the side of her face.

I check to see where she is at in her labor, and see the head of the baby still in place. I ask Delphine to let me know when she has her next pain, as I will try to gently pull the baby while she is pushing, and hopefully, this joint effort will result in the baby being delivered.

"The pain is coming back," she tells me loudly.

"I am going to count to three and on three I want you to push just as hard as you can," I tell her. She nods her head, her face glistening from all the work she has been doing.

"One…two… *three,*" I shout. Delphine bears down, as I place my hands gently by the babe's head. There is a sound like a suction, as the head slides into view, and I gently ease the head forward and out. We wait a few minutes for the next pain, and the shoulders come out as well. One more contraction should be enough to push the baby out. I do not have to wait long, as Delphine pushes again, and a slick baby slides right into my hands, with a noisy wail. I clutch the baby to me and check to see what sex it is, then bundle it into a blanket to present to Delphine.

"You have delivered another girl," I tell her as I hand the baby to her to hold. Delphine puts her arms out and hugs her new daughter close to her. While she is doing this, I wait for the afterbirth and then clean Delphine up as much as I can. Nanny and I move her over a bit, so we can tidy her and make her presentable to her husband. Once the area is cleansed, which doesn't take long because we're experts at it, we call an anxious Everett in to see his new daughter.

Nanny and I leave the room to give the parents some time together with Evaline, while we have a drink of water, and tidy ourselves.

"Another quick and healthy delivery," I say to Nanny.

"Yes, Delphine is very fortunate," she says. Midwives and helpers are always relieved at easy and live births. Joy is always so much more preferable to grief.

Everett comes out after a short while with a large smile upon his face. I pass him and return to the room to see how mother and daughter are doing.

Delphine smiles at me. "Thank you for helping me again," she says to me.

"It is my pleasure. And I am grateful it all went well," I tell her, walking over to give her a kiss.

"I will be heading home, as I know Nanny will take great care of you."

"Good night to you, Mercy, and thank you again," she tells me, then returns her gaze to her daughter.

I retrieve my bag and walk back into the kitchen, where Everett and Nanny are waiting.

"Goodbye Nanny. Congratulations on your new granddaughter," I tell her.

"Thank you, Mercy," She replies with a large smile as she walks back to the room I have just left. She will be staying for a while to help Delphine with the new baby and older children. Like I said, she is indeed a blessing.

"Congratulations to you as well, on a healthy daughter," I tell Everett.

"Thank you Mercy, and let us be on our way so you can get a few hours of rest before your own brood is up and about," he replies.

We walk out into the dark night and climb back into the wagon, to return me home.

Tuesday, March 8th, 1886

It has been nearly one year since my twins have passed.

A year without them bursting into the room like a herd of buffalos.

A year since I have reached down to accept a handpicked bouquet of flowers from them.

A year since I have enjoyed a hug from their little arms, and a year since I kissed them.

In the past year, I have become stronger than I thought I ever would be. I have helped others with losses similar to my own and cried myself to sleep at night missing them. I struggle some days to realize they are truly gone. I had them such a short time, yet they have left such a gaping absence in my life. Losing not one, but two of my children seems a cruel punishment.

Why would God need them more than me?

I do not know, and most likely I will never know the answer to that. Instead, I try to hold onto their memory. I try to remember their scent, their sounds and the feel of their little hands in mine. To comfort myself I steal glimpses of my living children as they sleep. Or play. Sometimes I simply watch them existing. I want to hold them tight and keep them close to me so nothing will ever harm them, but I know I cannot do this. I must live for the day, and hope they will all live healthily and happily past my time on this earth.

My one hope is never to go through such pain again. Aren't two losses enough? I fervently hope so. I have held these thoughts within myself all winter, knowing the season of illness will be upon us soon. I dread this time even more than last year, because now I know firsthand what can happen, and how it feels. In the month of the anniversary of their deaths, I seem to hold my breath in anticipation. And worry.

Let this month pass with all my children beside me, not sleeping in the cold, damp ground of our own family cemetery.

Please.

Sunday, May 23rd, 1886

It was a long winter, and I spent most of my evenings embroidering in front of the fire with my children playing at my feet, which was a lovely way to pass the time. My latest finished sampler is a small one that will go in our privy. It carries a verse saying "May you have joy wherever you go" with flowers surrounding the words. I loved the saying when I first saw it and thought it humorous as it applies to life as well as using the privy. I am not quite sure anyone else will get my humor, but it at least makes me smile and is indeed a pretty decoration for our privy.

The children are getting bigger, Mary Alice is now four, Maud Ella is three, and Charles is just over one year old. I have not become pregnant again, and I am fine just enjoying the healthy family I have. Once you lose someone you love, you truly appreciate the ones that are left in your life. I am also hopeful that I have had enough sorrow in my lifetime, and will only have happy times ahead of me. But sadly I know none of this is promised, so I simply carry on moving forward, hoping there is only joy in my future.

Gibby is outside harnessing Smokey to the wagon, and when we are ready to join him we stride across the yard over grass that lies flat at our feet, but is starting to turn green with the warmth of spring.

As we walk I notice at once that we are missing two boys running circles around us, and I try hard not to be morose on such a fine day. At my slow pace with the little ones, we finally reach the ever-patient Smokey and Gibby.

I look at Gibby to see if he too notices the absence of our little boys, but he just looks at me and smiles, his smile hiding any sorrow he may be feeling. I take his lead and smile back at him, then turn to pull myself up and into my seat. Once Gibby is in his familiar place he yells to Smokey, and with a lurch we are off and out of the yard, turning up the hill and leaving our home and our sad memories behind us, at least for a few hours. It is a warm spring day, and I tilt my face skyward, hoping the sun will warm my insides as well.

We arrive at church in good time, and as always wait our turn to drive in and find a spot to park our wagon. Gibby finds a place toward the back, and once we are stopped, he helps us to disembark. I hold baby Charles while he carries Maud Ella. Mary Alice holds his hand as we walk to the church entrance. The church has a sizeable crowd today, and we find our usual place toward the back, hopefully far enough away from the annoying tithing man.

I think back to how worried I was when my little boys attended… would the tithing man discipline them? Would they behave during the sermon?

Such trivial things now. I'd give anything to have them beside me again now, no matter how they behaved. It is a wonder the things you find important after something as serious as death visits your life. I shake my head to clear away these somber thoughts and place a kiss on little Charles's head. The clergyman begins his sermon, and I listen intently.

Saturday, June 26th, 1886

It is a warm evening in our home, and the Culvers and the O'Dowds are over for a visit. It is as though our friends are rallying around us to lift our spirits.

We have finished dinner, and Cora, Delphine and I are sitting on chairs from my kitchen that the menfolk have kindly brought outside for us. Our sewing bags are at our feet, as we all sew together. The sun is starting to set, and we are hurrying, trying to get some last stitches in before the light fades and we have to put our projects away for the day.

I am working on a quilt that will contain some of the twins' clothing so that a part of them will remain near me.

As we work on our respective projects, I look up to see that the girls are following the boys as they look for fireflies. The insects are just starting to show their tiny beacons of light as the yard darkens with the sun slipping away behind the trees. The children run about, trying to guess where they will see a firefly next. Seeing them run along the edge of our yard reminds me of two other children that loved doing this, and I sigh.

"Are you feeling all right, Mercy?" Cora asks as she and Delphine look up after hearing me exhale so deeply.

"I'm just thinking about the twins and how much they loved catching fireflies. I wish they were here to join in," I answer with a catch in my throat. Often times my grief will rise up like a wave that catches you unaware at the beach. You think you're safe, then suddenly it soaks you.

"We wish they were here as well," Cora tells me, and both women look at me with concern etched on their faces. Wanting to move on from my sadness, I change the subject quickly.

"Have you heard any gossip from town?" I ask my friends. Since we are not in the company of the sewing group tonight. It's just us three, and we don't mind a bit of salacious talk. I also know what I say will not travel further than our little group.

Happy to oblige and change the mood, Delphine starts to speak.

"It seems like Bertha Jones is at it again," Delphine says, smiling as she speaks.

"She's taken up with George Devlin this time," Cora tells me. There are some people that you just don't like no matter how hard you try, and Bertha is one of them. When you speak to her, she will cock an eyebrow at whatever you say, and then tell you exactly what she thinks. A few years ago she disagreed with me and took to yelling at me during a public picnic. I steer clear of her at all events now. She is a bit of a shrew and not well-liked – except by some of the menfolk. She enjoys the company of other ladies' husbands, going around like a cat in heat. She is a short, heavy woman with large breasts that she exaggerates with her dresses, like a shopkeeper showing off her wares. I have personally seen her husband leaving a local tavern alone, distancing himself from the pain she causes to him and to wives throughout the town.

"That's honestly not such a bad match. I guess they deserve each other!" I exclaim. George is well known for the way he mistreats his animals. Many of us have seen it for ourselves, watching as he whips his oxen to push them harder when hauling a large load. Once when he was stuck in the snow with his team, he whipped them so viciously the snow went red from their bleeding. I'm happy that these two dreadful people have found each other, although I feel some pity for their long-suffering spouses. I wonder what it must be like being married to such ghastly people! I think of Gibby, and I smile, pulling myself out of my reverie of the twins.

"I'm not surprised those two found each other," Cora says. "It would be lovely if they left town together! They're creating quite a scandal riding about town in George's carriage, and we personally have seen them up on the hill at nightfall."

Delphine gives an emphatic nod. "I doubt they're reading the bible parked up there in the field," she says. At this, I join in the laughter, and it feels very good. Very good indeed.

Tuesday, July 13th, 1886

We are on one of our usual trips to town, traveling along Pine Hill beside the great wall when we see a bizarre sight! In my friend Cecile Pendleton's yard is the undertaker's hearse! You'd think this would be unusual, but actually it's not. There are some pranksters in town who are always stealing Mr. Bates's hearse and leaving it all about town. I am thankful that whoever these rogues are, they never leave it in our yard. I have seen quite enough of that hearse, thank you!

It takes a bit of effort to perform this prank, and I am surprised that whoever does it hasn't been caught yet. Whoever it is has to bring a horse, harness it, and then drag it off to wherever they are going to park it. Maybe there's a group of them and they pull it themselves. I am assuming it is not a large group, as this has been going on for a few years and I cannot imagine that a crowd of people could keep a secret that well. What is the saying? The only way two people can keep a secret is if one of them is dead.

Either way, as we're heading to Whitford's we see the large black hearse on Cecile's grass. I see her and her husband outside, talking with the undertaker, who is known to be a bit grumpy. I can't really blame him considering that he has to chase his hearse all over town! The poor man has enough to do dealing with the dead and their grieving families.

This hearse has appeared at the Cider Mill during cider season and in the field before the 4th of July fireworks. It has even made it as far as Voluntown a few times. Often people know who it belongs to, and return it to the undertaker themselves, but sometimes he has to go looking for it. I can imagine it is quite an inconvenience for him Mr. Bates is quite lucky this time, as he lives a stone's throw away, so he didn't have to travel far.

I love a good prank myself, but I am not sure I can enjoy this one, as it would give me quite a fright to see the hearse in my yard.

As we pass we see Cecile and her husband waving at us, and we wave back as Mr. Bates hitches his horse to the hearse in readiness to take it home.

Friday, August 27th, 1886

What a lovely summer we have had. Warm days alternating with just the right amount of rain, and the crops have grown at an astonishing rate. Gibby is pleased, as he won't have to depend so much on peddling firewood and other items in order for us to survive. We may even have some extra to put aside for savings this year. What a blessing after all our trials to finally have a good season and good health.

I am hosting a sewing evening at home tonight, and many ladies have attended. I can't say that we get a lot of embroidery done on evenings like this, it is more to seek advice and for the companionship. It can get right lonely at times not seeing anyone but your husband and children for long stretches at a time, especially during the winter months. Not everyone is as fortunate as me to have two good friends that visit often.

So while the weather holds, we are enjoying weekly evenings that will hopefully see us through a long winter. We share recipes to feed our growing families, gift one another samplers we have finished, and share gossip. It is a wonderful time indeed, and very vital to all us womenfolk who have so many chores and such little idle time.

For this evening's meeting, I've made some cookies to share with the ladies, and I am looking forward to seeing them all.

They arrive soon after supper, some traveling together, and we total eight in all. There is Delphine and Cora, Ophelia Piasecki, Lily Maleski, and Alice and Cecile Pendleton.

Most of the ladies have young children and are happy to gain an evening's respite with some female company. It is a lively group, and we retreat to my parlor where I have placed all the chairs I have along with a bench from the kitchen table as well.

Everyone takes a seat, empties their bag, and starts to organize the project they are working on. Some are working on samplers or quilts, while others have more intricate projects that look more like artwork. As we are stitching we talk about the latest news from town. A local mill closed last year, and many families are currently struggling, so we discuss how we can be of help to those less fortunate, especially with the harsh winter months to come.

"Perhaps we can see what clothing we can donate as well as food," Cora suggests. It is a fine suggestion, but families like ours don't have much extra clothing as we save it for future children, and even when they are beyond wearing the clothes become rags or even part of a quilt.

"We can check with the church to see if they also have anything that might help," Ophelia says.

The talk changes to the recent wedding of our President Grover Cleveland.

"That must have been quite a wedding at the White House last month," Ophelia remarks. She is quite worldly, and comes from a wealthy family. She has traveled extensively and even knows French. I look to her often for her knowledge, and for her suggestions on how to present myself. She has wide eyes, brown hair and a round face that typically has a smile upon it. She is fiercely loyal, but if you anger her, she will cut you off immediately. I hope I always stay on her good side, as I enjoy her company. Her husband is a lovely man named Felix, with bright blue eyes like a fall sky. He is very handsome and kind-hearted, and they make a lovely match.

"It's a scandal," Lily retorts. "He's 49 and he's married a 21-year-old! Twenty-eight years younger, she is! He was guardian to the bride after her father passed and now he's married her."

I do not say a word at those comments, and Cora with Delphine look at me. You can see by looking at Gibby and me, that there's a fair difference between our ages, too.

My parents knew Gibby and approved of the match, but I know that not everybody looked upon it so favorably. It was not uncommon for young girls like me to marry older men, as so many young men were lost in the war. But that time has passed now, and it is not very fashionable to marry someone with such an age gap.

My husband and I are also 28 years apart in age, and Gibby married me when he was 42. He was a wealthy sea captain, and had no time to get married when he was younger. Amassing quite a savings, my parents were pleased when he approached them to ask for my hand, even though I was only 14.

I drop my head and look intently at my quilt. I do not want to tangle with Lily or make her feel bad. I know exactly how it feels to put my foot in my mouth!

"I'm hoping to travel to New York soon. I have been wanting to see the Liberty Statue in person." Ophelia swiftly changes the subject, glancing my way. "I believe it should be finished by the fall," she says.

"My in-laws arrived in America by ship, and I can imagine the statue is quite a sight for those arriving, even while it's still being built," Ophelia says.

The Statue of Liberty is a gift from France and is currently being built in the New York Harbor. It has been a struggle to get it built, as the French wanted it to be a collaboration between them and the American nation. We Americans were tasked with financing and building the very costly base, and it was a slow process. Joseph Pulitzer, a wealthy publisher in New York City, has been using his paper to inspire people to donate even the smallest amounts. The funds needed have finally been raised and the pedestal on which Lady Liberty will stand is waiting patiently for her. I would love to see it as well, but I am not as financially stable as Ophelia, and I will have to be satisfied with hearing about it from her or seeing a photo in the papers.

"I am sure she will be quite the sight, standing tall with her torch welcoming immigrants and the like to our country," Delphine replies. Her family is from New York as well, and she is well familiar with the city.

"How are you faring in your new home, Alice?" I ask her.

"Very well, Mercy! I am still amazed at the generosity of our town. Your quilt is on my bed and looks lovely, as well as keeping us warm at night. You have a nice strong stitch and an eye for color." She praises me, which makes my cheeks feel warm.

"I am so glad that everything's going well for you, Alice, and you are enjoying my quilt so!" I reply happily.

As the evening goes on, the ladies become more comfortable and start to gossip.

"Tonight on our way here, I saw George Devlin's carriage parked up by the edge of the woods near Ekonk Hill. Do you think perhaps he was playing cards with Bertha in there?" Lily says with a giggle. All of the ladies except Cora came to my home by way of Ekonk Hill, so the more observant of them would have seen the carriage and would no doubt have nudged the others and pointed it out.

"Maybe they were playing Strip Jack Naked!" Ophelia says and we laugh uproariously at the salacious image.

"Earlier this spring they got stuck in a field near my house, and George knocked on our door for Felix to help him get out of the mud," Ophelia tells us laughing. "Felix was more than happy to help as he did not want to see George whip his horse. He got our team and pulled the carriage out. Bertha stayed inside the carriage, but poor old George got mud all over him!"

The room is filled with laughter while we continue to work on our projects.

"That woman has no shame, being seen all over town like that!" Lily says, shaking her head.

Gibby comes into the room while we're all laughing and smiles at us, and I see a glimpse of his teeth through his mustache and beard.

"What are you ladies finding so entertaining?" he asks, hoping we will share our gossip so he can join in the laughter.

"We were talking about how George Devlin seems to get his carriage stuck all the time, and in the most remote areas!" Ophelia says, chuckling, as we all join her. Gibby chuckles as well.

"That carriage never seems to make it as far as Hell Hollow, which is something I am quite thankful for," he replies. I know he heartily disapproves of George, especially in his care of animals. As I always say, you can tell a lot about a person from the way they treat animals.

"I wanted to remind you ladies that it is getting dark, and you may want to be on your way," Gibby says with a smile. We often need his reminder, as we lose track of time on evenings such as this.

At his words, I hear chairs scrape against the floor and the sounds of gowns swishing as the ladies stand and pick up their sewing bags, preparing to leave.

It was a wonderful evening, and it is nice to know I have such good friends in my life.

Saturday, September 25th, 1886

We're standing in our yard under a wide blue fall sky, waiting to board our wagon for a ride to the Rounds Cider Mill on Woodland Road. The apple crop has been abundant this year, and Mr. Rounds has been busy making regular cider as well as hard cider and even vinegar.

We have a little extra coin from our profitable harvest, so we are treating our family to some apple cider from the mill. Mr. Rounds often presses cider on the weekends, and customers can watch the cider being made right in front of them. We have witnessed this process ourselves in the past, but as our children are all quite young, we will just be stopping by to purchase some cider, rather than spectating. The children won't take a lot of interest in watching juice squeezed from apples – but they will enjoy the delicious treats made from it.

We're soon on our way, the wagon rolling along smoothly under the bright leaves and cerulean sky. It is a typical fall day, and I love the bright colors of fall, although I have a hard time enjoying them, knowing that the iron grip of winter is following right on fall's coattails. I shiver, thinking of cold snow piled up against my house, filling my walkways, and I hope we have a mild winter this year.

We soon arrive at the cider mill, which is not far at all, and we see that others have arrived there before us. Apple cider is a treat, and we aren't alone in wanting to purchase some. I look over and see the Culvers are here as well. Gibby guides our wagon right alongside them. They have just arrived, and we all alight from our wagons and hug each other hello. Mary Alice and Maud Ella run to meet the Culver girls and they grab one another's hands. Delphine is carrying her youngest, Evaline, and I am carrying Charles as we all start walking toward the cider mill.

A large barn looms in front of us, with the cider mill inside. One side of the barn is for the finished product, and the other side is set up for pressing. In between this, there is a viewing area for people if they want to watch the process happen. There is also an area containing shelves to hold the cider that has been made.

Customers bring their jugs back for more cider once they have emptied the contents, which means that the Mill has enough jugs for everyone.

As we approach, we meet Mrs. Rounds, who is outside greeting her visitors and collecting money for Cider. I suspect she is having a profitable day from all the activity we are witnessing.

"Good afternoon Mrs. Rounds," we say to her. She greets everyone arriving with a large smile. She and her husband are known to give much of their cider away to those in need, and there are many in need this year due to the mill closing. I am proud and happy we are one of the families who are able to purchase a jug of cider, and not have to depend on the generosity of others.

Making the cider is a lengthy process in which the cider makers pick out different varieties of apples, some sweet and some bitter, to balance the flavor. They wash the apples, then the apples travel along a chute into a grinder. The crushed apples drop onto a cloth-covered frame below, where workers spread the mashed apples and fold the cloth, keeping the apples inside. The workers then remove the frame and place the wrapped apples under a steam-driven press. The juice from the pressed apples trickles down into a tank where it is then bottled. This cider makes delicious doughnuts, muffins and other items, which sell out rapidly. It's a real treat to enjoy anything from the cider mill and bakery, and something I look forward to every year.

We retrieve our cider, along with a few apple and cinnamon doughnuts, and then head to the apple orchard area where there are a few benches. We sit here for a while and let the children run around while we adults sip our cider, eat our doughnuts, enjoy the beautiful day and the even better company.

Everett and Gibby talk about Gibby's harvest and Everett's quarry, while we ladies discuss school and our children's latest achievements. Before we know it a couple of hours have passed, and Maud Ella is clinging to her father to be picked up.

"Looks like it's time to go home," I say to Delphine.

"I agree. It was such a treat to see you and your family and spend the afternoon with you all," Delphine responds.

"Let's get our families together again soon," I say to her, leaning in for an embrace. We slowly walk back to our waiting wagons, while the girls run beside us, except for Maud Ella, who is fast asleep in Gibby's arms.

Saturday, December 25th, 1886

It has been a long and delightful holiday. Both of our parents came to our home for the season, which was very rare indeed, as they hardly visit together. Our families are both from Exeter, Rhode Island, which is a way to travel, especially in the winter months. So it was very enjoyable they came all this way to see us. They brought some gifts for the children and a lovely cake for dessert.

It is evening now, and I have my feet up on my little stool while my children play at my feet. I take a moment to savor the sound of my children talking and giggling, and the background noise of Gibby snoring in his chair. A typical wonderful family evening in my home.

Monday, July 4th, 1887

It's the annual July Fourth celebration in our town, and I am celebrating inside as well. Our family has made it through the winter with everyone healthy and happy. They are beside me, and they are alive. I feel as though I can breathe again, and relax just a little. Perhaps as time goes on this ache will ease more. I hope so because the feeling catches me sometimes and its almost too much to bear.

I am making a rhubarb pie to bring to the picnic, using a recipe from Aunt Babette's cookbook. I still haven't made the twins' favorite royal ham sandwiches, and I doubt I ever will again.

I have a little garden in our yard right outside my door where a large shrub of rhubarb grows, as well as spices and herbs for cooking. This morning I cut a few stalks of rhubarb, and I'm in my kitchen preparing the pie. After cutting the stalks into bite-sized chunks I put them into a bowl and pour boiling water over them, leaving them to sit. While they are softening in the boiled water, I prepare the crust from a starter dough I have on hand.

I strain the water from the rhubarb, then sprinkle it with corn starch, sugar and the juice of a lemon, then place it over the bottom layer of pastry with some butter. I cover the rhubarb with more crust and brush the top with a beaten egg. I then bake it in my oven, and although my kitchen smells heavenly, it is quite warm seeing as it's a hot summer day. Once the pie is cooked, I set it on an upper shelf in my kitchen. Not only do I not want my family eating it, I also do not want any of them to burn themselves on the hot dish.

I do all this in the morning so we can take the pie with us to the festivities later today. Gibby plays with the children while I make the pie, and I hum as I work, happy to be baking for my family. I make pies a few times a week, to the delight of my family.

We eat an early supper in the warm afternoon light, so we can head into town for the independence gathering. I clean my kitchen and table from dinner while the children play in the parlor. Gibby leaves us to harness Smokey to the wagon, and we are soon on our way to town.

The wagon rolls along leisurely, and a soft breeze caresses our faces as we travel. We see a few neighbors along the way and wave hello as we pass by. Soon we arrive at the field where the festivities are, and find it filled with parked wagons and activity. Children are happily running around, and folks are sitting in the evening sunshine on colorful blankets, while others take a refreshing swim in the nearby river. Gibby guides Smokey to where the wagons are stationed and pulls the reins to stop him. We both climb down and then help the children down as well. The second their little feet hit the ground they are off and running, so excited to see all the activity. Gibby takes our blanket from the back of the wagon as I take my pie, and we head toward everyone, looking for someone we know to spend our time with. As we are walking, I see Cora and Delphine waving excitedly, and we head toward them and their families.

"Hello, ladies!" I say to my dear friends, and they stand to say hello and embrace me. I put my pie down beside their food, and we sit together on one blanket, while the children run around nearby, playing together.

Gibby leaves our blanket with me and heads back toward the wagons and horses where the men are smoking cigars and talking together.

We ladies chat about the usual subjects—what our children are doing, recipes and any gossip we may have heard.

"I hear that Bertha and George got scared by screams near the grave of the British Soldier," says Delphine.

"What British soldier?" I ask her. I am not from this area, so sometimes I need to be enlightened.

"There's a small grave on a trail off Cedar Swamp Road, and it is said that the ghost of a British soldier roams the woods looking for the man who killed him. People have heard screams, and it looks like Bertha is the latest," Delphine informs us.

"That sounds like a good enough reason for me to stay away," Cora says with a grimace.

Shaking my head, I speak. "I don't believe any of it. I wish people would just let the dead rest in peace. Someone loves these people and misses them, and you get your just rewards if you're out cavorting with someone else's husband and get spooked by a spirit."

My friends nod their heads. I've heard a few legends or tales in our area myself, but I never believed them. I always think that these ghosts had family once, and were loved. If indeed they had a violent ending, they should be left in peace. Maybe if more people minded their own business, these folktales would just fade away. I can only imagine how the families must feel when they hear about such legends. I would never want a family member of mine's memory or final resting place to be tortured so. I think of the twins in their plot in the field and a cold wind comes at me through the warm evening. A wind it seems that only I can feel. A second later and it's gone.

Cora changes the subject, and we talk about what we are working on for our latest sewing projects, and the afternoon flies by. Before we know it dusk arrives, and our husbands and children join us on the blankets to watch the firework show.

Gibby sits with Mary Alice nearby, while I lie back on our blanket with Maud Ella and baby Charles on each side of me.

The show lasts a while, with fireworks filling the sky, bursting and sparkling above us, and I am content. Smoke from the fireworks acts as a canvas, reflecting the lights and colors, making the sky very bright. Suddenly there is chaos in the sky as light, color, and explosions sound the finale. A lone firework like a shooting star trails to earth, and the show is over.

As the last firework fizzles out, we rise from our blankets and gather our families to return home. Gibby carries both Maud Ella and Charles, while I carry the remnants of our pie and blanket. Poor little Mary Alice stumbles alongside me, too tired to walk, but having to because she is the oldest, and most able. Thankfully it is a short walk to our wagon, where Smokey is pawing at the ground, ready to leave.

Gibby lays the blanket out so the children can lie on it and sleep for the ride home. He sets them down on the blanket, where they curl up with one another, intent on sleeping.

It is a pretty ride home, with moonlight guiding our little wagon. The road is fairly busy as other families return home alongside us. The further we get out, the fewer wagons there are until there is only us traveling along. By this point it has become quite dark, and Gibby stops for a moment, jumps from the wagon, pulls a box out in front of his seat and lights the lanterns on the sides of our wagon. When he's done, he returns to his seat beside me and gives me a big smile that I can barely see for the long mustache and beard that covers the lower half of his face. I return his smile, and he then flicks the reins for Smokey to continue pulling us home. Smokey's hooves are the only sound we hear, a steady rhythm that keeps the children sleeping.

At one point a carriage comes towards us, and as we pass Gibby tips his hat to the driver, who is none other than George Devlin. I glance at his passenger, and although it is dark, the silhouette looks to be Bertha Jones. I do not wave as we pass, as I have no wish to be kind. I wonder what story they tell their spouses when they return from their outings. Oh, the shame of those two!

As we are roll down the hill into our hollow, I see a glimmer of light, which is the glass from our windows shining in the moonlight. Smokey knows he is close to home and picks up his pace, as anxious to be home as I am.

Monday, September 5th, 1887

Mary Alice is now old enough to begin school. We had no illness last year within our home, which makes me wonder if it was because no children attended school from our household, and nobody had the chance to catch anything. I would love to keep her and all my children at home with me, but I know I cannot stop them from learning and attending school. It would be selfish of me. Oh, but how I struggle with this.

Gibby insists she goes, and I know he is right. So on a bright September morning she joins Cora's children and attends her first day of school. I pack her a lunch and give her a slate that was Earl's to use, and off she goes. I try not to worry. I have lost two children, and surely death cannot strike my family yet again.

Mary Alice enjoys her day and comes home bubbling over with news of all the friends she has made and the plans for the school year. Mr. Wood is still teaching at the Wylie school, and I wonder if he recognized her surname. The twins would have been seven years old now and they had thoroughly enjoyed attending school. I try to change my thoughts as they will quickly make me terribly sad.

Instead, I think of how lucky Mary Alice is to be attending school at a schoolhouse so close to our home. It helps to try to find positive points, because to think about everything the twins are missing is heartbreaking. I hope with all my heart they are the only two children I lose, as two children lost is quite enough heartbreak.

Friday, September 30th, 1887

The dreaded diphtheria has returned to our little town, as it seems to always do. I try very hard not to live in fear, but I am failing, and fear has me deep within its grip. I have three healthy children remaining and I am sick with worry that I may lose one.

There have already been a few deaths in town, and I have decided that Mary Alice will stay home from school for a while in the hope that it will protect us from the illness.

Monday, October 3rd, 1887

I have been too late in keeping little Mary Alice away from school. Either that or she caught an illness from somewhere else. Either way, Mary Alice is quite sick. Time will tell whether it is diphtheria or not, and I pray not.

Gibby sleeps in the children's room with them, while Mary Alice sleeps with me in my bed. I hope that I will be able to protect them by keeping them separate. It is the same as it was with the boys…swollen and sore throat and a fever. I have no recourse but to do the same as I did with the boys. A wet washcloth to try to break the fever, broth for the congestion, and lots of rest and love. I pray it works this time, as I cannot fathom the idea of losing another child.

It does work—at least for Mary Alice. Like a miracle she wakes one morning and tells me she's feeling better. I weep with relief. She is smiling and happy, and being an astute child she knows full well the joy we are feeling at her recovery. We let her go back to her room with the others, and I cannot believe how lucky our family has been. I fall into bed that evening with Gibby, exhausted from taking care of our daughter and the worry it caused. We cling to each other, happy and relieved that our family has remained intact.

Tuesday, October 4th, 1887

The bright sun streams into our bedroom, waking me from a deep slumber. I take a minute to enjoy the peace of the morning, then fling back the covers and rise from the bed. Gibby is snoring lightly, exhausted as I have been from taking care of sick children. I get dressed quietly and walk to the children's bedroom to see how they are faring. Mary Alice is sleeping peacefully as is Charles. But Maud Ella is flushed with fever, tossing and turning.

My heart skips a beat. I blink my eyes hoping when I reopen them it will be a different scene, and all three of my children will be sleeping peacefully. But when I reopen my eyes the same distressing scene is in front of me. Two children are fine, but another has taken sick. I take Maud Ella from the bed and run back to my room and Gibby.

"Maud Ella has a fever!" I yell to him.

Gibby looks at me with wide eyes and sits up in the bed. He is exhausted as well, having taken care of the younger children while I nursed Mary Alice.

"Are you sure, Mercy?" he asks me.

"I most certainly am," I respond. He stands and starts to get dressed, while I return with Maud Ella to the children's room. I wake Charles and Mary Alice gently and tell them to get up and go to their father. I see them drop down from the bed and then leave the room as I asked.

I lay my youngest daughter down on the bed, and as I do so she wakes and looks up at me through glassy eyes. Gibby comes into the room with our water pitcher as well as some cloths so I can try to break her fever. She lays there, and I hope that the rest and the cool cloths will heal her.

Gibby is wonderful as always, taking care of the other two children. I am blessed with my friends as well, as Delphine and Cora stop by with food so neither Gibby nor I have to cook.

I spend my time with Maud Ella, reading to her and trying to break her fever. Her throat swells hugely, causing my worries to escalate. I rarely leave her side, and the hours turn into days. She is much sicker than Mary Alice was, and I am beside myself.

Gibby brings me food that my friends have left, but I can barely eat it. I cannot believe I could lose a third child to this terrible illness. How is this even possible? Many others have not even lost one child, why am I to lose three? It is unfathomable.

But it happens.

After a few days of sleeping next to Maud Ella and taking care of her, she is finally starting to improve. I am relieved that my labors have helped, and tiptoe from Maud Ella's room, leaving her sleeping peacefully.

Gibby is sleeping with the other children in our bed, so I head to my comfy parlor chair and fall into it. I lift my feet onto my little stool and fall asleep in an instant in the dark parlor. I am exhausted but filled with hope that my daughter will indeed continue to improve.

Light streams in on me, waking me, and I jump with a start, realizing I have inadvertently slept past my usual time of waking.

I take a moment to listen, but my house is still silent as everyone sleeps on. Stretching my arms up, I rise from my chair and head to Maud Ella's room, hoping that she is feeling even better after a restful night of sleep.

I reach her side in the big bed my children typically share and I cannot believe what I see. My little girl is blue. Her eyes are shut as though she is asleep, but she is stiff. She is a corpse. I shake her, but she is cold to the touch, and I know that there is no hope.

I wail, and turning to leave the room to wake Gibby I step on something left on the floor. I lift my skirt to see what I have stepped on and see an apple, or at least the remains of an apple half eaten, and I can see bite marks where Maud Ella's teeth have broken the skin.

How did she get an apple? She must have gone into my kitchen and taken one, as we have not been giving her anything but soup. In her hunger, my little girl went and fetched an apple. And that apple killed her when she choked on it.

How did none of us hear her? Especially me, in my chair in the parlor, the next room over.

Knowing what has happened I go back to her and sit her up, shaking her, trying to restore her to life. I cannot see from the tears blurring my vision, and I hear someone sobbing.

I feel hands on my shoulders, and I realize that Gibby is behind me, trying to hold me back and stop me from shaking Maud Ella. My beautiful, precocious little girl is gone. Another child has left me too early.

I lie with her lifeless, cold little body until the undertaker arrives, and at that point they have to pull her from me.

As the undertaker takes her away, I see the apple again where someone must have kicked it. It has rolled against the wall. I grab it, sobbing, and take to our bed.

My pillow is soaked from my tears, and my eyes are almost swollen shut. This time it is harder to rise from my bed after losing my daughter. When the boys passed, grief was new, and the intensity was something I had never experienced before. This time I know what will happen and I know where my daughter will lie. With the agony of my loss comes the certainty of the gaping hole that will be in our home now that she is gone from us. Like someone has simply taken her away and stolen her from the room, never to be seen again.

Delphine and Cora alternate sitting with me, trying to console me. I lose track of time and days, and I no longer have the will to live.

I wake one morning with Gibby beside me, and see the forsaken apple at my bedside, shriveled now and brown. I rise and head to my kitchen and look through my shelves and cupboards. I finally find what I am looking for—a plain glass canning jar. I twist the cap off and carefully drop the apple core inside, then put the cover back in its place. I add alcohol to preserve it and then I return to my bedroom, place the jar on the little table beside my bed, and lie down next to my sleeping husband.

Saturday, October 8th, 1887

I wake this chilly morning alone in my bed, as Gibby has been sleeping in the children's room. He is struggling as well, and cannot get any rest with me sobbing for most of the night. I know it is selfish, and I know that he is hurting as well, but I cannot think of anyone but myself at this point. As I become more awake, I notice someone is in my room, sitting beside my bed.

I recognize my visitor as Cora, and I roll over and look at her.

"Good morning, Mercy," she says to me.

"Hello Cora," I reply.

"You have to get ready for the service," she tells me.

I roll away from her and face the window, where I can see the canning jar and the apple. My daughter's toothmarks are all that remain of her.

"Mercy, you don't want to miss saying goodbye to her, and if you do not get up you will do just that," Cora tells me.

I lie in the same position and let the silence fill the room.

"Please Mercy," Cora says.

It is those softly-spoken words that propel me forward. She is right, I don't want to miss saying goodbye.

I have given it a lot of thought, and I do not want her to be buried with her brothers in our sad little family cemetery. I want her buried in the grove in the pine trees on the knoll above my house, where I can see her every day. Burying my twins so far away was a mistake I do not want to make again.

I move to the side of the bed and rise to a sitting position with my back to Cora. The room is silent, and I am sure my friend for once is at a loss for words. What words could possibly exist to soften the blow for a friend that has not lost one, nor two, but three of her children?

I stand and walk across the cold wooden floor to my wardrobe, where Cora joins me, and we pick out my black funeral dress together. How awful is it that I am once again to wear it at a funeral service for one of my children?

She helps me out of my nightgown and into my chemise, and then into this dreadful dress that I decide I will burn after this ceremony. Maybe if I don't have a mourning dress I will never have the need for one again?

Could it be that easy?

These thoughts run through my head while I sit on the edge of my bed as Cora braids my hair and pins it into a bun. While she is doing this, Delphine enters the room, her face contorted with sorrow. She looks to the table on the side of my bed and sees the canning jar holding the apple and does not look surprised. I am sure Gibby has told my friends about it, but at this point no one wants to ask me why I am keeping the morbid, terrible apple that robbed me of my daughter.

Delphine comes to my side and she and Cora put their arms around me, holding me between them. I am enveloped in their love, and I take a minute to appreciate my dear friends coming to my side. We stay like this for a moment, until I hear footsteps come into my room. It is Gibby carrying Charles, with Mary Alice following. They are all dressed for this morbid occasion

"Gibby, I've changed my mind about Maud Ella's resting place," I tell him. Cora and Delphine look surprised, but to their credit they say nothing.

"You have? Where did you want her to lie?" He asks me, raising his dark thick eyebrows. I can tell that he's trying not to be frustrated with me.

"I would like her to be buried up on the knoll above our home, in the clearing. I can look up to her resting place whenever I want. The twins are too far away, but I didn't give it much thought at the time. Now I have more experience with death, I would like to have her closer to me." I respond.

He looks at me thoughtfully. "The grave has been dug already at the family cemetery," he says firmly.

"A hole can be easily filled, but my wishes are the same. Please place her within view of our home," I ask of him.

Gibby is a man of few words, and he does not often have to strive to understand me. But he does try to placate me whenever he can, and I can see that he is struggling.

The preacher will be arriving soon, along with the mourners, and now he has another grave to dig.

"Please." I look at him and mouth the one word.

He looks at me and turns from the room and leaves without a sound. Mary Alice and Charles are left behind, which makes me believe he has gone to carry out my wishes.

Cora and Delphine sit quietly with me for a while on the edge of the bed. The children climb up to be with us as well, and we sit like this for a few moments, even the children realizing the gravity of the moment. We rise together and walk through to the kitchen, the children following.

I look out my kitchen window and see Gibby, Everett, and Jasper digging a grave on the hill for my little girl. I sob again and turn to my friends.

Cora and Delphine gently guide me from my kitchen, and through the back door to the outside.

It is a dreary day, of which I am very glad. I turn to the right, and my friends flank me on both sides. Cora carries Charles, and Delphine holds Mary Alice's hand. We walk this way, three abreast with the children, up the hill to the little knoll that now contains a freshly dug grave. A little coffin lies near it, with the men standing alongside and a preacher nearby.

I also see the outlines of other people, but in my desolation I cannot focus on any of them. I reach the forsaken site with my friends beside me and stand silently while the preacher starts the ceremony. It is like the boys' ceremony, where I hear words, but I cannot relate to their meaning. I hear someone sobbing and realize that it's me.

My hands are held tightly by my friends. They stand close to me, bracing me, as they hold me up. Once it is over, I bend and place both hands on the coffin, and pause. This is a moment I cannot savor. I cannot get any respite from it, but it is a moment I will remember forever.

After a few seconds I turn and walk away, with my friends at my side, but then I stop and turn back to Gibby.

"Please come with me and let our friends do the rest," I ask him.

"I can't do that, Mercy. Just as you took care of her in life, I have to tend to her in death. I need to see it done properly," he says.

I have no response to this, so I kiss his cheek and then turn and walk down the hill with my remaining children and my friends beside me. We walk back to my home, which now has one less child within.

Monday, November 21st, 1887

It has been a month since Maud Ella passed. Yet another little one has been taken from me too soon. I miss her soft little voice, her light brown curly hair, her eyes wide with wonder at some newfound thing. The apple core is preserved and sits on my kitchen windowsill, with her solitary grave in the background. The apple is brown now, but her teeth marks remain, and I can still see them well. I imagine her little teeth in a smile on her face. I try not to cry and I usually fail. How could anyone not cry at the thought of a child taken too soon?

I see her grave as I prepare my family's meals. I see her grave when I tidy up from those meals. I see her grave when I close my eyes to sleep. Her grave is sheltered by a grove of pine trees, which drop their needles to cover the grave in a velvet blanket. It is a tranquil spot, and being close to our home makes me think of her even more—which may or may not be a good thing.

Mary Alice is thankfully doing well. She misses her sister, but asks for her less and less now. Charles Adam has taken the loss of his sister more easily. He is too young to know what it means.

I have recently discovered I am with child, so there is hope yet again. But I'm scared this time. Childbirth is so difficult, and to lose the child a few years later seems intolerable. How will I bear it? I have no choice either way, as this babe will come whether I like it or not. It is due to enter this world next May, around the time of what would have been Maud Ella's third birthday.

I am so thankful for my remaining children, who push me to go on. They need me to take care of them and to love them. Some mornings I can hardly lift my head off the pillow thinking of my precious twins and my little girl. But then I hear the patter of little feet entering my room, and the soft word "Mama", and I know I am needed. And this need is what propels me forward and pushes me on.

Sunday, December 25th, 1887

Another Christmas season is upon us, the second without our rambunctious little boys and the first without Maud Ella. Both my parents and Gibby's came out again to our home for the holiday, which is a wonderful new tradition I am enjoying. My father says he comes for my delicious apple pie, but I know he is also concerned about my sadness over the loss of my children. I am fortunate to have such considerate parents, and Gibby's parents are supportive as well. It is a busy holiday as always with lots of food, gifts, and family.

It's two months now since little Maud Ella passed. Two months of not seeing her little figure following close behind Mary Alice. Two months of missing her soft little voice asking for her favorite cookie, missing her little hand in mine as we walk together. This is my third loss and I do not see it getting any easier. It's as if my heart has been torn from my body once again. I wonder sometimes how I even get out of my bed. And then little Mary Alice arrives at my side, and I know how I must rise. Thank goodness for my other two children who need me so much. They give me the strength to go on.

Life is like a river. There are days you float along happily, the sun warming your face, the water cooling your body. You are relaxed and at peace. Then there are times where the current is rough, you are thrown about, and it's difficult to keep your head out of the water. You gasp for air as you pop above the surface, then you drop back down again and there's comfort in the darkness as the waters take you. It's easier than staying afloat, and trying not to drown. But float I must, as there is a little girl checking in on me, shaking my shoulder, pushing my hair from my face, anxious to see that I am well.

I think these thoughts while I sit at my kitchen table, with the parents sitting around me, as well as my immediate family. It is noisy, as everyone is talking at once, and there is the sound of silverware on plates, the clink of glasses being picked up and put down. The normal sounds of life. Sometimes it is very good to just enjoy the normal. And to be thankful for it.

That's what I am doing this Christmas. I am savoring it all. It seems that when you've lost so much you are wary about when the next loss will happen. I look at the faces around my table and it's hard to not worry over who will get sick next. Or whether the crop will be bountiful this year. It seems there is always something to fret about, so I will enjoy this moment for what it is.

A happy, healthy family enjoying the holiday together.

Monday, March 5th, 1888

The dreaded month of March has arrived once again. It is a month I wish could be stricken from the calendars, eradicated from the year. Even Caesar knew to beware of March. Diphtheria returns to our little town every March, and every year that I don't lose a child to it is a relief now. I am especially grateful this year as we had it tear through our little town this past winter.

I count all my remaining little ducklings, and I thank the Lord that they are still here by my side. It gives me hope, and I hope as I always do that my luck continues.

Both Charles and Mary Alice had birthdays this past February. Charles is now three years of age, and Mary Alice is now six.

Mary Alice loves school and does well. I take turns with Cora bringing the children back and forth to school like we always have. Sometimes the routine is a good thing—it pushes you, it forces you through long days of sorrow. My enlarged belly also reminds me of how life goes on, as I have another little one arriving soon, possibly late May or early June. It is hard to tell with me, as they typically arrive early, which is fine with me, as the last few weeks of a pregnancy are always very tiring.

I fear I may have made a mistake in placing little Maud Ella's grave so close to our home. Seeing it every day seems to prevent me from healing.

Gibby has taken the jar containing the apple from my window ledge in the kitchen and has buried it at her gravesite, much to my sorrow. But perhaps he is right in doing so. How can I heal with so many visible reminders, when I have enough scars inside me to remind me of her?

As well as losing Maud Ella last year, we had a terrible harvest. A poor harvest means less food and coin for our family, adding to our never-ending struggles.

The state of Connecticut has approached us out of the blue, looking to buy our lands and make them part of a public forest. Gibby and I are pondering their offer, as it might be worthwhile to make a profit on our land.

Cora and Jasper have already sold their homestead and will be moving away next month. I have been helping her pack when I have the time, but I'm not much help in my condition. I dread her leaving, as once she is gone it will be just our little homestead and the ghosts of my departed children.

I know I will miss Cora sorely, and Mary Alice will miss her and the O'Dowd boys. For now, we still share taking the children to school, but that will change when they leave Hell Hollow. Soon we will be alone here, and after three deaths the place is starting to live up to its name.

From my warm bed on this dreary morning, I watch the raindrops run down the glass of my window. I watch as a single raindrop skirts another, then another, and finally joins another drop to travel together further down the glass. There's strength in numbers, I think. Normally I love a good rain. The rain leaves new color in its wake, especially in the Spring. It brings nourishment to trees, the flowers, and even the people. But today's rain does not renew or replenish me. It makes me even more mournful. The raindrops dripping down my window pane match the tears cascading down my face. The rain reminds me of my misery. My grief.

I turn from the window and bury my head in my sheets. I hear the soft patter of feet, and the bed dips down a little as Mary Alice climbs upon my bed. The mattress sinks as she nestles in beside me and rubs my back. I try to wipe my eyes, so she does not see me crying, but she is very intuitive and I'm sure she knows. I pull the sheet away and smile at my lovely daughter. She and the others help me to put both feet on the ground, stand, then walk to face my day. I know they need me. So I cannot wallow in my self-pity knowing others in my little family depend upon me. It is good to be needed.

"Good morning Mama," Mary Alice says softly.

"Good morning Mary Alice," I respond, moving away gently so I can get out of bed.

"You are up early for the day, are you excited for school?" I ask her.

"I am!" She exclaims, as it is getting on for the end of the school year and she is happy about this. "Soon I'll be home every day, and I can help you more," she says, smiling.

"I look forward to having you all to myself," I smile back at her, returning what I hope she will think is a happy smile.

She jumps from my bed and runs off to get ready for her day. I am grateful for her interrupting my sadness this morning. She reminds me that I am still blessed with her and Charles, and another baby due soon. I am always reminded that no matter how much loss I have had, life still goes on. It travels on without the boys and without Maud Ella, and one day it will travel on with or without me.

Times are changing quickly, and we may decide to leave our little hollow. I am starting to feel that with the loss of my three children, and the difficult farming, it may be time to move on. But I am torn about leaving my departed children in their lonely graves, and the idea of going or staying becomes a vicious circle, spinning in my head. Gibby is conflicted as well, but this harvest season will decide him, I am sure. We have been here for quite a few years now, and we've all put in a lot of work, with not much success. The only thing we have in plenty is memories of loss.

I dress for the day in my usual pregnancy attire, and walk to the kitchen to start breakfast. I walk with my shoulders thrown back to counterbalance the weight in my belly. It's ungainly, and I know it. The days are all the same lately, and thankfully the new babe will change things a bit, which is a good thing indeed.

Gibby will take Mary Alice to school, as in my condition I cannot go far these days. With Cora and her family busy with preparations to leave, I am alone more often, and will only have Delphine to help me when I give birth. I hope that my lying in goes as well as it has in the past.

I can only hope.

Monday, April 16th, 1888

The Connecticut State officials have called again. It seems our homestead and the lands that go with it are in a crucial spot, and they are anxious to have it. The State has had the foresight to think about putting aside land for future generations, and this land will be a forest for people to enjoy. There will be no homes, no buildings of any type, just open land, like it was before man arrived. Gibby has been deep in thought these last few days and I have also told him my true feelings about leaving Hell Hollow as well. I am anxious to leave here and start somewhere new.

Perhaps a new beginning and fresh start would be good for all our family.

I am cooking in my little kitchen, which is, as always, in the shadow of my daughter's grave. As I cut carrots for a stew, I look through the window to see her grave under its canopy of pine trees.

I would dearly love to look out a window and see something else. I can carry their memories easily enough in my heart.

I think about all three of my departed children enough, and this grave so close to our home wears on me. I finish cutting the carrots and put them in the pot to join the rest of the ingredients for tonight's dinner. Gibby has been at his never-ending chore of cutting firewood and will be returning home soon.

Gibby does indeed return shortly, and we sit at our table to eat the stew I have prepared for dinner. We listen to Mary Alice as she tells us about her day and how one little boy had his knuckles rapped at school today for misbehaving. After her lengthy story, Gibby puts down his spoon and looks directly at me.

"I believe I have come to the same conclusion as you, Mercy," he finally says.

"And what would that be?" I ask, trying to keep the hope from my voice.

"That we should leave this hollow. The state is as anxious to have it, and I know you're anxious to leave it too. I have struggled hard to make a living here, and getting a good harvest is a never-ending battle. The soils just aren't good enough to farm. If we take the State's money we can move to an area that would be better for us all. We could buy a new home in a place that's already proved to be productive. But most of all, it would be a fresh start for us all. In a place with no memories," he finishes, looking earnestly at me.

As Gibby talks, Mary Alice looks at me, then at her father, then back at me with concern on her little face. My poor little girl has been through as much as the rest of us these past years, and my heart aches to see her worried.

"Papa, could we stay near my school so I could carry on going there?" She asks.

"It depends on what properties are available," Gibby replies. "I've already started looking, and I've spoken with the fence keepers to see what properties are for sale. There is a house very similar to our home down the road in Voluntown. It has fields with good soil, and it's proven to provide food and a living for a family. It may be a godsend. The State wants to buy our land and it will give us the chance to make a new start."

I put down my spoon and just listen, filled with happiness that my husband is willing at last to leave this home.

"When can we look at this home? And can we afford it?" I inquire of my husband.

"We can afford it, and there'll be money left over. The State is being pretty generous, and I think we should take their offer. If we do, we will have to move quickly, as I would like the new baby to be born in our new home," he says.

"I am happy to move whenever you like!" I say. It's all I can do not to run around the table and hug him. "I like the idea that the new baby will be born in the new home. I just hope we can do it in the time I have left. I'm due in early June, and I don't know how much help I can be right now, so we don't have much time."

"We'd best make a start, then," Gibby smiles. "I'm sure we can do it, but we'll have to visit the home immediately and start proceedings so we can move in time. I guessed you might like the idea, so I've actually made arrangements to visit later this evening, if you are up to it." Gibby tells me. His smile brightens his face and goes right to his eyes now. His long beard quivers a bit as if the smile has tickled it.

"I am ready as soon as we clear up from dinner," I respond. I stand, picking up my bowl and utensils to bring to our washing area on the counter, and Mary Alice follows with hers. Soon we've washed everyone's dishes, and left them on the table to dry.

Since it is only April and still a bit cool, I ask Mary Alice to fetch sweaters for her and her brother, while I walk to my room to gather something warm for myself. All bundled up, we walk outside to join Gibby in the side yard. He is bent over hitching Smokey to the wagon, and when he's finished, he loads the children into the back. I pull myself up into my usual spot with his help, as is not an easy move with my large belly.

"I am grateful I can still make it in my condition, as I am looking forward to seeing the home you're looking at," I say looking at him with a broad smile.

The wagon shakes as he joins me, and Smokey smoothly pulls the wagon forward. Gibby directs him to the right at the end of our driveway, going down the hill rather than up it as we usually do. As we continue down Hell Hollow Road, he points out all the land purchased by the state.

"What is the state doing with all our property?" I ask him.

"They'll take it down and make the whole neighborhood a public forest. No homes or businesses will be built here, although our family cemetery will be protected. People will be able to hunt, hike, and enjoy the open land," Gibby informs me.

"There's already lots of open land, so I wonder why they came up with such an idea to save more of it from being built upon. It is definitely an interesting idea," I respond. I'm used to open woods and enjoying nature, but there are many people living in rented mill houses, or in the cities that don't have this kind experience.

"I don't know who came up with it, but I am happy because the offer has come at a great time for our family," Gibby says.

The sun hangs low in the sky and the trees rush by as we travel towards our possible new home. Smokey has such a smooth gait, and before I know it Gibby is pulling the reins to stop him, as we pass a pretty white house that looks just like mine but a bit larger. There is a small barn and lots of open fields adjacent to the farmhouse.

A large lilac bush grows at the side of the front door, not yet in bloom, as if it's waiting to welcome me to my new home. I love lilacs and it's a wonderful omen that there are already some established here.

Gibby comes to my side to help me down, and we all walk together to the front of the house. Gibby raps his knuckles on the door, and soon an older gentleman appears opening the door to us.

"Hello, Mr. Reynolds," he says to Gibby with a large smile.

"Good evening, Mr. Hopkins," my husband replies. "This is my wife, Mercy. I've brought the family to look at your home."

"Hello Mr. Hopkins," I reply returning the man's smile. Mr. Hopkins is an elderly man with a kind face and a lovely smile that shows straight, white teeth. His head is covered with white hair, and he wears suspenders in the fashion of most men these days. A newsboy hat sits atop his head, giving him a jaunty look.

Moving aside from the door, he waves us into his home, keeping the large smile upon his face. We proceed through the open door and into a large hall with various rooms leading off from it.

Bright sunlight filters in everywhere, making the home bright and full of light, even though the sun is setting. The light colors in the home make it cheerful and inviting. I instantly love it.

I walk into the parlor, where pretty wallpaper of light colored flowers lines the walls. This is a treat that I would not be able to afford. I always love a cheerful house as my parents' home while I was growing up was full of Jacobean stained wood, leaving the house very dark. I have always tried to avoid having anything dark in my home.

I am quite relieved that the farmhouse is better than I expected as there is enough work to be done relocating our family, never mind also fixing the new house to our liking.

Mary Alice peeks around my skirts shyly and looks at Mr. Hopkins.

"Hello, Mr. Hopkins. Could you please tell me where my room will be?" she asks him shyly.

"Well, my dear that would be for your parents to decide, but if you follow me I think I might have one you will truly like!" Mr. Hopkins says with a smile to Mary Alice.

Mary Alice removes herself from the safety of my skirts and takes her brother's hand and leads little Charlie forward to follow Mr. Hopkins to her possible new bedroom.

Gibby and I smile at each other and fall in behind them. The house is almost the same floor plan as our own, except it is a bit fancier, with lots of wallpaper and a finished upstairs floor. Depending upon how many more children we have, a second floor with additional rooms may come in handy.

Mr. Hopkins walks back down the hall to the staircase and starts walking up. We follow and he shows us the three bedrooms on that floor. We discover a large room to the left, which would most likely be for Gibby and me, and then two smaller ones to the right. A fireplace in the larger bedroom will give us warmth in the winter and help to heat the home.

We move down the hall to the two smaller bedrooms, and as we enter we discover there is more wallpaper in a lovely floral style with large pink cabbage roses climbing the walls. I feel as though I have entered an English garden. I look at Mary Alice and she is grinning from ear to ear. This room was made for my little girl!

"I think this would be a wonderful room for you, Mary Alice, and how nice it will be not to have to share with your brother as well!" I tell my happy little girl.

Mary Alice looks around and then walks to the one window in the room which overlooks a tree, with the fields behind it.

"That is an apple tree, Mary Alice. It has such pretty blooms in the spring, and delicious apples in the fall. It would be a truly pretty sight from your window." Mr. Hopkins tells her.

"I just love it all!" Mary Alice exclaims with a smile so large I worry she will split her face in two! It is wonderful to see her so happy.

We leave the room that will almost certainly be Mary Alice's and walk across to the other small room, which is painted a light robin's egg blue. It is almost uncanny how perfect this home is for our family.

Now that we have seen all the rooms upstairs, we go back to the first floor, and when we reach the entry hall, Gibby looks at me and raises an eyebrow as if to see what I think. I greet his look with a smile and nod my head to show him that I am happy with it, and he turns to Mr. Hopkins.

"My wife is pleased with the looks of your home, Mr. Hopkins, and if the offer still stands we would very much like to have it," Gibby tells him.

"May I ask why you are leaving such a fine home?" I ask him.

"Of course you may! I am older now, and I can't take care of the fields—nor do I particularly want to. My wife passed last year, and I've been getting lonely. When I sell this place I plan to go live with my daughter at her home in Rhode Island. She has some room for me, and I would like to end my days with her and her family. I have many wonderful memories here, and I would be happy knowing that another family is enjoying this home once again. Filling it with lots of activity and joy," Mr. Hopkins says.

"We would be more than honored to live here and enjoy this beautiful home," I tell him.

Gibby reaches out his hand to Mr. Hopkins and they shake hands, cementing the deal. The talk then turns to finalizing the purchase, and we discuss the possibility of moving in before the latest baby is born.

"I am truly sorry for your losses, Mercy. My wife and I lost a babe to diphtheria as well. It is so very hard to lose a child. My wife struggled with the loss her whole life, as I am sure you do as well."

"Thank you, Mr. Hopkins," I respond quietly. He is certainly correct that the grief never goes away. But even with his reminder of my loss I feel happy inside, as I feel as though I have come home.

While Gibby and Mr. Hopkins talk about farming, I venture outside to see more of the yard.

It is a lovely yard, with a good sized privy off to the side. There are no flowers surrounding it, so one of the first things I shall be doing is to plant some to mask the smell on warm days. I feel grateful there is not much else that needs to be done.

The sun finally dips below the horizon as the men come outside to join the children and me.

"We need to get the little ones home," Gibby says to the older gentleman.

"I remember those days well." Mr. Hopkins says with a smile. "Let's see what we can do to get the new babe born in your new home." He tells us, looking at me.

"That sounds excellent," I answer, and we start toward Smokey and our waiting wagon.

The sunset above creates a pink glow that reflects from large billowy clouds.

It is a perfect ending to a wonderful day.

Monday, May 28th, 1888

I straighten up from placing my dishes in the cupboard and look at the view from the window of my new kitchen. The window looks out over a long field, with the apple tree in the foreground. Mr. Hopkins told Mary Alice that the tree is lovely when it blooms, and he was correct, as it's blooming now, and it is indeed a beautiful sight. I think back to my previous home with a view of my daughter's grave and it makes me pause. I often wonder whether I did the right thing in moving from my children's graves. Was I selfish in doing so? I surely hope not. I think of them enough each day, and the sight from that window was too much of a reminder for me.

I love and miss my children dearly. That will never change. But life is for the living, and my living children need me at my best. And seeing that reminder every day was overwhelming. I am also thankful that the whole area is to become a park, as when I am dead and gone, who knows what new owners might have done with her and the boys' graves? Not everyone is respectful, and this move ensures that they will rest in peace. At least I fervently hope that they do.

My new kitchen is now filled with my own things, and the sun streams through the many windows of the house, filling it with light and hope.

It has been a dreadfully long month. Once Gibby and I decided to leave Hell Hollow, it was nonstop work packing our belongings. There was so much to pack and move from the house and the barn, as well as a few of our other outbuildings. Gibby traveled to our new home daily to ready the barn for Smokey, Bessie and our other animals.

Since Mr. Hopkins is going to live with his daughter he has been quite generous, leaving us some of his furniture and other household items. I am so overwhelmed with gratitude. He is like an angel to our family.

Mr. Hopkins is happy that his beloved home is going to a young family, and we are grateful to have it.

"Mama, can you help me please?" Mary Alice interrupts my thoughts as she enters the kitchen.

"Yes, Mary Alice, what do you need?" I ask her.

"Can you please help me with my bed?" she asks. Earlier I helped her make her bed, as we are sleeping here tonight for the first time. Throughout the day she has continually asked me to go to her room on the pretext of helping her with something, and I suspect it is because she is a bit nervous about being alone in our new home and having her own room as well.

"I surely can," I say, and with that I follow her down the hall, up the stairs, and into her pretty room with the cabbage roses climbing the walls. As I suspected, the bed is fine, except for one small area that's been pulled out. I fix it, and then give her a big smile.

"Isn't it wonderful that you have a room all to yourself, and such a lovely room at that?" I ask her.

"Yes, and I love the tree!" she exclaims, walking over to the window to gaze out at it.

I walk to her side and place my hand on her shoulder as we gaze out together at the lovely sight from her new bedroom.

A tree in full bloom, a new home and a healthy daughter standing next to me. Life moves on with or without us, and I am glad I made the decision to move forward with it.

Tuesday, May 29th, 1888

The sun streams through the windows of our old parlor, the window panes creating long rectangular shapes across the floor, empty rectangles now, as there is no rug or other household item for the light to fall upon. I look around the empty house and it looks pretty worn now. The home served us well.

It kept us warm and dry during storms, and was mostly a happy place full of laughter and love. But sad memories can ruin or overcome wonderful ones, and sadly that's what happened here.

This is the last time I will be in the first home I shared with my new husband. The home where I gave birth to five babes and lost three of them. The home where I had lots of joyful memories, but also such terrible loss.

I walk slowly around the house one last time, to make sure that it is indeed empty. I hear my footsteps echo loudly on a floor that's barren of rugs, toys, furniture, and most of all my family. My steps bring me into my kitchen, now bare of our table and cook stove. The shelves no longer hold my bowls, plates, utensils and other things. As if under a spell, I walk toward my window, and look out the clear glass panes one last time. I immediately see my daughter's shaded resting place up on the knoll, glowing as usual with the orange pine needles that have fallen and created a blanket over her while she sleeps.

I think as I always do of my departed children, and say a short prayer that she and her brothers are at peace. I am grieved to leave these children behind, yet I know selling our homestead will mean that our land and the neighboring acres will become a new state forest, guaranteeing that my departed children will always be protected by the land they lived, played and died on. That no buildings or places will be built near them or over them. There will only be the wind and sun above them, animals roaming around them, and birds flying peacefully overhead. The land will eventually go back to its original state. There will be no more open fields with flowers blooming to pick and place upon their graves. No tall grasses will sway when the wind whistles through. Trees will grow, seeding their own generations when they drop their acorns or pine cones, and birds will do their part to carry these seeds, helping to create this new woodland. A new wilderness that will carry no trace of my children. Or of my family. Or of me.

One day, instead of seeing a stone wall within a field, we will instead see a mature forest shading their resting place. The woodland will grow quietly and slowly around them, protecting them.

Our house's stone foundations, its stone walls that once marked the limits of our property, and the white cross marking my children's resting place will be all that is left to show that our family was ever here. One day people will come to this new forest and not even know there are three children resting within the woods.

They will be forgotten.

I shake my head to clear it of these morose thoughts and take one last glance out the window. The knoll where Maud Ella rests glows still, as it always will. Perhaps I am wrong, and that one day the future generations of my family will walk these woods where we also walked, and stop for a moment to pause and think of their kin, resting beneath the ground. I sincerely hope they will take a moment to think of us, and these dearly loved children that passed so heartbreakingly young.

I change the direction of my thoughts to how very pleased I am, that our new child will arrive in this world in our new home, and hopefully find a much luckier beginning.

The moment is broken as Gibby calls my name. I take one last glimpse through the window and turn away to walk to the side door that leads me out to my family waiting in our wagon. A wagon that will take us all to our future in our new home.

EPILOGUE:

December 13th, 1909

Lydia stood on the boardwalk at New York Harbor, admiring the large imposing statue across the water. The cold breeze ruffled her long brown hair, and she smiled at her new husband standing beside her.

"I wish Momma and Mary Alice were here to enjoy this view. Momma donated a bit to the cause and always talked about the progress of her being built," she said to Jessie, turning her head once again to the beautiful sight of the Lady of Liberty overlooking the harbor.

"Maybe we can get her out here one of these days to enjoy the view. Until then, let us enjoy it ourselves and bring her something back as a souvenir, something that might inspire her to join us on a future trip." Jessie replied.

Lydia and Jessie had been married the Thursday before and were on their honeymoon in New York.

"I would love to take them with us on a future trip, and maybe Edward and Charles too," Lydia smiled as she spoke of her brothers to her handsome new husband.

Jessie stood close to Lydia and put his arm around her as they watched the setting sun change the sky from a lovely bright blue to orange, with streaks of bright yellow.

It was a fitting end to their honeymoon to see the statue her mother Mercy had spoken about so much and had longed to see.

At least one member of the Reynolds clan had made it at last.

I am the great, great-granddaughter of Mercy and Gilbert Reynolds, and I am very proud to be so knowledgeable about my family's history due to the wonderful record keeping of my father, Charlie Reynolds, Jr. In case you were wondering, Charles Adam was my great grandfather, and I was fortunate to meet his wife Antonia, who lived to the age of 102. How I wish I had asked her about Maud! I certainly missed out on an incredible chance to learn more.

It was my mother, Marilyn Reynolds, who made me such an avid reader, and I wish she was alive to read my first novel. I hope she would have been proud.

This novel was a work of love, and if you liked it, please leave a review on Amazon, or wherever you purchased it from. These reviews help self-published authors like me immensely, and we are always grateful when you take the time to leave a review.

Thank you for reading my book. I truly hoped you enjoyed it.

Acknowledgments and special thanks to:

Susan, Meredyth and Colleen, for reading the book and helping me to develop the story, and to Elaine and Christine for giving such accurate notes on what needed work.

Megan McCory Gleason for helping with writing and historical aspects,

Nicole Neiswanger for helping form the story,
Sherri Hirschboeck and Michele Perreault for help with editing,

And lastly my editor, Perry Iles, for polishing my words and making them shine brightly.

References

Town of Sterling Historian, Megan McCory Gleason

Roads lead back to Glory; a History of Sterling, Ct. 1982, Sterling Historical Society, Lead Researcher Carolyn Bailey Orr, a book about Sterling, Ct.

Sterling in Retrospect-Sterling Bicentennial Committee 1976, Written by Ruth Gallup

Michael Carroll for showing me Bert and Earl's graves and providing dates to help the story.

A glimpse into homesteading. Retrieved March 2021 from: https://iamcountryside.com/homesteading/simple-homesteading-life-in-the-1800s/

Information on the origin of Labor Day, Retrieved May 2021 from: https://en.wikipedia.org/wiki/labor_day

Information on the Statue of Liberty, Retrieved May 2021 from: https://en.wikipedia.org/wiki/Statue_of_Liberty

Information on the scandal with Grover Cleveland. Retrieved May 2021, from: https://news/americas-forgotten-presidental-sex-scandal-034111346.html

What happened in America in 1890s, retrieved May 2021 from: https://hhhistory.com/2015/08/what-happened-in-america-in-1890s.htm

American life in the 1880s, retrieved May 2021 from https://hhhistory.com/2015/05/american-life-in-1880s.html

Housing in the 1800s. Retrieved May 2021 from:
https://seducedbyhistory.blogspot.com/2009/05/housing-in-1800s-america.html

How to give birth (100 years ago), retrieved May 2021 from:
https://www.theweek.com/articles/454290/how-give-birth-100-years-ago

President Cleveland's Problem Child, retrieved May 2021 from:
https://smithsonianmag.com/history/president-clevelands-problem-child-100800/

Hats and bonnets history retrieved May 2021 from:
https://vintagedancer.com/victorian-hat-history/

History of fashion, retrieved May 2021, from:
https://glcp.uvm.edu/landscape_new/dating/clothing_and_hair/1870s_clothing_women.php

Days of the week calendar, information retrieved May 2021, from:
https://www.dayoftheweek.org

Kitchen stove information retrieved May 2021 from:
https://evolutionhomeappliances.weebly.com/kitchen-stoves-1800s-cast-iron.html

Aunt Babette's Cookbook, recipes retrieved May 2021 from:
https://d.lib.msu.edu/fa/4#page/196/mode/2up

Penny candy information retrieved May 2021 from:
https://truetreatscandy.com/the-first-penny-candies-whats-missing-and-why/

Horse and buggy information retrieved May 2021 from:
https://blog.newspapers.com/horse-and-buggy-the-primary-means-of-transportation-in-the-19th-century/

Diphtheria epidemic, information retrieved May 2021 from: https://collections.mnhs.org/MNHistoryMagazine/articles/15/v15i04p 434-438.pdf

Cooking in the 1800s information retrieved May 2021 from: https://ncpedia.org/culture/food/cooking-in-the-1800s

What people ate, a food timeline, retrieved May 2021 from: https://foodtimeline.org/foodpioneer.html

Prices for things retrieved May 2021 from: https://choosingvoluntarysimplicity.com/[rices-for-1860-1872-1878-and-1882-groceries-provisions-dry-goods-more/

Information about women and their right to vote, Retrieved March 2021, from: https://www.msn.com/en-us/news/politics/when-did-women-get-the-right-to-vote-in-the-united-states-a-timeline/ar-BB17RPgZ

Information about President Chester Arthur, retrieved May 2021, from: https://history.com/topics/us-presidents/chester-a-arthur

Information on Grover Cleveland's wedding, retrieved May 2021 from: https://people.com/politics/grover-cleveland-white-house-wedding-frances-folsom/

Information about life on a farm, retrieved May 2021 from: https://livinghistoryfarm.org

What early settlers ate, ask a prepper, retrieved May 2021 from: https://askaprepper.com/how-the-earliest-frontiers-preserved-food-and-how-they-fed-themselves/

How to make apple cider, retrieved May 2021 from: https://americanprofile.com/articles/making-apple-cider-video/

Made in United States
North Haven, CT
09 November 2021